I0525212

To Edward D. Hoch,
Who came close to batting a thousand.

Copyright © 2022 by DAVE CREEK

All rights reserved.

No part of this book may be reproduced in any form or by any electronic or mechanical means, including information storage and retrieval systems, without written permission from the author, except for the use of brief quotations in a book review.

THE SECRET OF PLAINSVILLE AND OTHER STORIES

DAVE CREEK

TABLE OF CONTENTS

INTRODUCTION BY
BILL NOEL

Enjoy a good mystery? If so, you're in for a treat. More accurately, not one treat, but thirteen treats skillfully created by award-winning author Dave Creek.

The collection *The Secret of Plainsville and Other Mysteries* will have you sharing a roller coaster ride with police charged with solving the most challenging whodunits. You'll be seated next to the dear, sweet next-door neighbors who ... you know, the ones you thought never could've committed the unthinkable. You'll be riding with good people doing bad things to avenge the past, to right wrongs. In the seat behind you on the coaster you'll find the person thrown into a hair-raising situation no one should ever experience. The stories, like the roller coaster ride during its slow, methodical trip uphill will lull you into a sense of calm. Then, well, you know what happens next. Hold on for dear life as the world falls out from under you, before jarring twists and turns slam you against cold, hard reality.

Like surprise endings? If so, Creek's *The Secret of Plainsville and Other Mysteries* will be right up your alley, that is if can handle what awaits you at the end of that dark, ominous alley where you'll not only be shaken by the present, but the past will rear its long-forgotten head. You'll learn how people not unlike you react when faced with moral dilemmas or no-win choices. You'll view the criminal underbelly from the eyes of those charged with solving the crimes; from the perspective of those committing the heinous acts; and, from the view of those caught up in the tumultuous, unpredictable world around them. Not only will you see events from those involved, you'll feel, truly feel, the raw emotions, the highs, the lows the fictional characters are experiencing. You'll ask yourself what would you do in similar circumstances while at the same time hoping you'll never have to make those choices?

As a writer of mystery novels, I'm keenly aware that not everything that looks good is good; not everything that appears evil is evil. The trick is telling the difference and telling it in time to save yourself and those around you. Creek does a masterful job of pulling you into the stories. I'm not saying *The Secret of Plainsville and Other Mysteries* will answer these thorny questions of good versus evil, but I assure you they'll be with you long after you finish the book.

No two of the stories are alike, but each share elements of surprise, mystery, intrigue, a dollop of humor, and pose questions for which there are no simple answers. Pull up a comfortable seat, take a deep breath, and let the adventures begin. You won't regret it.

FOREWORD

Stories of crime and suspense usually bring us characters dealing with deep distress. Perhaps they're facing imminent danger of being killed or severely injured, or a loved one faces similar danger. They may be falsely accused of a crime or fear that someone close to them is capable of, or has already committed, criminal acts.

Such scenarios are ripe for story possibilities, and for exploring various facets of a particular character. At times the surface plotting of such a story draws us in -- what's going to happen next, is someone about to die, will it resolve in a twist ending that I never saw coming?

But such stories, featuring characters under increasing pressure, can also provide insight into human nature, whether they portray Edward D. Hoch's resolute (often amateur) detectives painstakingly pouring over every potential clue to solve a murder or Joyce Carol Oates's determined survivors of sexual abuse and other forms of violence.

Normally I write science fiction, but sometimes my imagination brings me closer to home, generating a story where all the characters are recognizably human, and the settings are more familiar than a starship or a previously unexplored alien world.

As Bill Noel mentioned in his Introduction, many of the characters in these thirteen stories find themselves facing "moral dilemmas or no-win choices." That can be excruciating for those characters, of course, but I hope you, the reader, can find both entertainment and perhaps something to think about in these tales.

THE SECRET OF PLAINSVILLE

Your father dies taking a closely-held secret to the grave with him -- a secret your late mother also guarded zealously. In this story, I wanted to explore just how far a son would go to obtain answers he feared he didn't even want!

A smooth layer of snow already covered the cemetery's grounds. Thick clouds obscured the sun and obliterated shadows. Still the snow fell, and Richard Farrell found himself fascinated by the sight of individual flakes striking his father's coffin and instantly melting, their moisture running in ragged rivulets down its polished mahogany sides.

I used to love watching snowflakes coming down when I was a child, Richard thought. *But at sixty-two years of age, I just resent the cold.*

Richard and his sister Alice stood next to the coffin, the only mourners remaining. The funeral director activated the device that began lowering the coffin into the grave.

"There he goes," Alice said, her voice barely carrying in the still air, "and all his secrets with him."

Richard cupped his hands against his mouth and breathed warm air into them. "It can't have been anything that awful."

"You don't know that. Those mysterious trips. The money."

Every summer, their father Gene Farrell left the family restaurant and disappeared for a month. Their mother, Becky, remained at home, forever tight-lipped about those trips until the day she'd died, three years earlier. Each time their father returned home, he was exhausted, not refreshed as he might've been after a vacation. Even at age 87, thin and frail and using a cane, he'd set off on that year's journey. Two months after his return, a heart attack took him.

Richard took his sister's arm as they walked toward their car. Alice told him, "You should look into his records. Find out once and for all what he was doing."

"If you're that interested, you should do it."

Alice's mouth pressed into a thin line for a moment before she spoke: "Some of us still have jobs, you know. And extended family we actually visit."

"You don't have to -- "

"Richard, you've been retired fifteen years. What the hell is a 'strategy manager,' anyway? I don't know what you did then, and I don't know what you do now."

Richard held Alice's elbow as he opened the car door for her. "I made people a lot of money -- and, well, I was one of those people. As for what I do now -- I'm in no danger of running out of beer or out of movies to watch."

Alice mostly kept silent as Richard drove toward her home. As she was about to get out at her driveway, though, she said, "I understand if you don't want to do that for me."

Richard shook his head and held out his hand. "It's your obsession, not -- "

"It's not an obsession. And it's not because I'm the little sister Mom and Dad always wanted you to take care of. It's something we need to do. In Mom's memory." Alice slammed the car door closed before Richard could respond.

———

RICHARD STOOD IN THE BAY WINDOW OF HIS STUDY ON THE third floor of his home. He could just make out the still-falling snow against the silhouetted woods of the western side of his estate. A glass of wine from a bottle that he knew represented a week of Alice's salary at her insurance office sat untouched on a nearby table.

Alice had to bring up Mom, Richard thought. *Had to guilt me. Mom never spoke of Dad's yearly adventures, if that's what they were. Try to ask her about it, and she just waved a hand at me, like she was pushing my words away. Just turned her head and shut her eyes.*

What didn't she want to see?

———

A TURN OF THE KEY, AND RICHARD LEANED HIS SHOULDER against the door of Gene's Place to force the door open. The restaurant still stood abandoned two years after his father had shut it down. *Another chore I haven't taken care of,* Richard thought. *I should sell the place, even though I've never fielded a good offer.*

Behind him, the morning sun provided the only illumination, revealing dust motes filling the interior. Richard's nose tickled, and he sneezed. He fumbled for the

3

lights. The overheads blinked several times, as if reluctant to reveal the dusty floor and confused jumble of tables and chairs.

Richard kept moving, through the kitchen area with pots and pans still hanging from hooks, through the break room with ancient bags of chips and chocolate still in the vending machine, finally arriving at his father's office. More dust arose when he entered, and the lights were dim.

Once he stood before the large four-drawer filing cabinet he was never allowed to touch while his father was still alive, he had to chuckle at the tiny lock that was its only protection. *I know Dad kept a hammer around here somewhere,* Richard thought. He rummaged around his father's desk and found the hammer in the bottom drawer. A couple sharp strikes, and the lock fell away.

Richard sighed as he opened the cabinet's top drawer and saw just how stuffed it was with paper records, some tattered and frayed, some sheets white, some yellow, some red or blue. *And not a one of them in any order, it looks like,* Richard thought. He grabbed a mass of them at random, used a handful to sweep the dust off the desk, and sat down in the dim light to study them.

That first set of records he'd grabbed involved routine business transactions -- payments to employees, food vendors, maintenance workers, many others. Those exhausted the top drawer, and the two in the middle. He started to stuff the mass of papers back into their respective drawers, but he'd have sworn they'd expanded to half again their size once freed from their captivity. He settled for stacking them on the floor.

Richard took a deep breath as he opened the bottom, final drawer. *If these papers are more of the same,* he thought, *then my father's secrets went down into the grave with him.*

As he spread those papers onto the desk, though, his eyes widened and his heart raced. Hotel rooms, all in the same little town, the same time each year. *My father never travelled for business, and he and Mom never took vacations.*

The image of his mother waving her hand, turning her head, closing her eyes forced itself into his consciousness. *Sorry, Mom. Wave all you want. My eyes are wide open.*

RICHARD PULLED HIS RENTAL CAR INTO A PARKING SPACE IN the town square of Plainsville, Kentucky, a community of about 12,000 people about 75 miles southeast of Louisville. The sharp rays of the mid-afternoon sun made him squint, and the chill air made him grab a light jacket as he got out and examined his surroundings. *Pretty typical small town,* he thought, *or at least what I imagine such a town to be. Brick courthouse, check. Cupola, check. Big clock, check. Real Back to the Future stuff.*

A brief walk around showed him a number of small businesses that lined the square, mostly craft stores, clothing stores, and a scattering of restaurants, most of which seemed to specialize in "country cooking." None of them was his destination, though; instead, he sought a place called "Bhaava," which had received hundreds of thousands of dollars of his father's money across nearly seven decades. Using his father's records as a basis for investigation, Richard had traced those funds through several accounts belonging to shell companies supposedly located in several states, in reality residing only within an elaborate financial fiction. One of those accounts contained enough investments to keep a steady stream of money funneled toward "Bhaava," whatever it was.

Richard made nearly a complete circuit around the square when he found an empty storefront with a handwritten note on the door: "Bhaava has moved." The new address was printed underneath.

Richard peered into the abandoned space, hoping to get an idea of what it had been devoted to. Other than a couple tables and a broken bouncy chair for infants, he couldn't make anything out. *One block east, then,* he thought, *and headed that way.*

As he made his way out of the square and down the street, though, his pulse raced and breathing quickened. *This could be the moment. What will I find out about my father? What will I have to tell Alice? Did he go see a lover in this little town each year? How could such a relationship have lasted into his eighties? Cancel that, I don't want to know.*

Could it have been something else he would've been ashamed of? Drugs? Prostitutes? Seems unlikely. Or is that wishful thinking?

Soon Richard found himself in front of a sprawling, two-story Victorian home. The only indication that he'd reached his intended destination was a small sign over the front entrance that said "Bhaava" in elaborate script. As he walked up the steep stairs, onto the porch and toward that entrance, a middle-aged woman opened the front door and asked, "Can I help you?"

Richard blinked a couple times as he fought for words. "Uh -- I was just interested in the kind of work you do here." He waggled a finger at the overhead sign. "I'm not familiar with that word."

The woman looked at him through narrowed eyes. "It's Sanskrit. For 'being' or becoming.'"

"Of course it is."

"My name's Patricia Gunther. Are you here to volunteer?

We have plenty of positions available, and we always need more help."

"What kind of positions are they?"

Patricia stood straight and folded her hands. "Well, we can always use more people in the daycare. Our homeless shelter can use cooks or servers."

"Greeters?" Richard asked.

"Yes, of course. We show our customers to a table, take their order, and serve them as anyone would at a regular restaurant. Just a matter of showing respect to people who are trying to get back on their feet."

"I see."

Patricia tilted her head. "Somehow I don't get the impression you're here to volunteer. Just what is it you want?"

"Look, I'll just tell you straight out. My name's Richard Farrell. I'd like to -- "

Patricia gasped. She held a hand up. "You stay right there," she said as he retreated into the house. "I'll have someone here to talk with you in just a minute."

Richard could only stare at the door as he waited. A sharp breeze blew dust in his eyes, and they watered. As he was rubbing the moisture away, he heard a new voice: "Mr. Farrell?"

A man close to his own age stood in the doorway. "Yes," Richard said. "I'm Mr. Farrell."

The man stepped forward to shake his hand. "I'm Elliot Johnson. I'm the director here."

"Oh, very good. Did you know my father?"

Elliot took a deep breath. Rubbed his chin. Told Robert, "Why don't you come inside and we'll show you what our facility is all about?"

"Fair enough," Richard said, and followed Elliot inside.

A long hallway ran straight toward the back of the house. Wide doorways revealed large rooms to either side. Elliot indicated the first doorway to the left. The room was filled with infants and toddlers, some playing with balls or trucks or dolls, others napping in cribs or on mats. Several women, most of them looking to be grandparent-age, were playing with them or simply watching over them. "This is our daycare," Elliot said. "Most of the parents were recently homeless. We train them for jobs, but they don't make enough to afford daycare. This helps them get by in the meantime. We help people for several counties around."

Computer workstations filled the first room to the right. Most of them were occupied by older pupils mostly being instructed by younger people. Elliot explained, "This is where a lot of our success stories gained computer skills that let them return to the labor force -- or in some cases, enter it for the first time."

Elliot stopped halfway down the hallway. "We have satellite facilities in other parts of town. Older teens who dropped out of school or wouldn't ever have a chance to go to college are learning auto repair, plumbing, electrical maintenance, any number of skilled trades."

Richard said, "All this is well and good. But it's all been financed by my father, is that correct?"

"It has. And we were very sad to hear of his passing."

Richard kept his voice low. "I appreciate that. I hope you can appreciate that his survivors -- my sister and I -- knew nothing about all this until I looked into it after his death."

"Oh, my," Elliot said.

"Please understand, in just these few moments that you've shown me around, I see the worth of what he did. But the secrecy surrounding it disturbs me. I want to know the reason behind it."

Elliot shrugged. "That's not something I can speak to you about."

"'Can't or won't?'"

"Can't."

"And why is that?"

"I can't tell you that, either."

Richard said, "You realize that as executor of my father's estate, I can cut off the funding he provided."

Elliot favored him with a wan smile. "You should also know that we have funding to prevent that, as well. Legal resources."

"You'd fight me on that? What was Dad's big secret? That's all I want to know."

Elliot indicated the front door. "I'm afraid it's time for you to leave."

Richard tried to stare Elliot down, but the other man's expression didn't change. Finally Richard said, "All right. I'll see what I can find through other sources."

"I wish you luck, then," Elliot said as he escorted Richard out.

———

RICHARD RETURNED TO THE TOWN SQUARE AND ENTERED THE courthouse, quickly finding the court records office. He hesitated a moment just outside, then girded himself and went in. A couple clerks worked at computer stations while another behind them filed documents away. He made a quiet cough, and the woman doing the filing turned, smiled, and asked, "How can I help you?"

"Let's hope you're able to," Richard told her. "What I'm looking for might be several decades back. I'm looking for any information I can about Gene Farrell."

The clerk leaned against the counter, arms spread wide. "May I ask why?"

"Simple reason. I'm his son."

Richard could've sworn he heard the woman groan. "I'm afraid we wouldn't have any information about him."

"Really? You know that without looking."

"As you said -- that information goes several decades back. We never transferred records that old to our computers, and the paperwork is long gone."

"Perhaps the local police might know something. I'd like to talk to the chief."

"You can try. But I don't think she'll want to talk to you."

"Fine," Richard said, and left without another word.

RICHARD HAD A QUICK SUPPER AT ONE OF THE COUNTRY cooking restaurants on the town square, then checked into a bed-and-breakfast just a couple of blocks distant. He tore off a page of the room's stationary and sat, pen poised over the paper, considering a list of goals for the next day. *Talk to the police chief after all?* he wondered. *Might as well. There has to be a local newspaper, too. Maybe they have archives I can look through.*

Or maybe they'll blow me off like everyone else in town. It's just spooky.

The phone rang. Richard stared at it a long moment before he picked up the receiver. "Hello?"

A muffled male voice said, "So you want to know what your father did?"

"Who is this?"

"Be at the southeast corner of the abandoned warehouse

at the edge of town at midnight. You'll find out everything you need to know." The speaker hung up.

Richard stared at the receiver in puzzlement for a moment before he placed it back onto the phone cradle. *Yeah, right,* he thought. *Did whoever that was think I've never seen a crime show on TV?*

———

Damn, it's dark out here, Richard thought as he stood at the southeast corner of the abandoned warehouse just before midnight. The building was visible mostly as a dark presence that blotted out the stars. And I could use a thicker jacket. He stamped his feet and rubbed his hands together, while making sure to stick close to his rental car.

Richard's watch read 12:07 when he spotted the headlights coming down the access road toward the warehouse. The figures of two men were silhouetted in the front seat. *These guys can't even be on time for their own appointment,* he thought.

The car halted just in front of Richard's, blocking its way. The two men, one short and rotund, the other tall and stringy, piled out of their car. They looked at one another and laughed.

Short Guy said, "Looks like you kept your appointment."

Richard tapped his watch. "But you're late."

Tall Guy nodded and smiled as he said to his partner, "He's a funny guy. I didn't know he'd be a funny guy."

Short guy said, "Shut up, Mike. Let's just get this done."

Mike, formerly Tall Guy, said, "Hey, you used my name, *Arnold*."

The former Short Guy, Arnold, shook his head. "I guess

we're even now." He turned toward Richard. "Listen, we didn't come here to hurt you."

Mike clapped a fist into his other hand. "Speak for yourself."

"Shut up, Mike." To Richard, he said, "We just want you to leave. This doesn't do you any good, and it sure doesn't do us any good."

Richard said, "This is all because of the big secret."

"It's because it's none of your damn business," Arnold said.

"He was my father, dammit!"

Mike stepped forward, fists clenched. "Enough talking. Let's -- "

A voice from the darkness: "Hold it right there!" A brief burst of a police siren along with flashing red and blue lights punctuated the outburst. Then an intense spotlight targeted Mike, Arnold, and Richard.

"Good to see you were really there," Richard said as he shielded his eyes against the spotlight's glare.

Plainsville Police Chief Karen Hildebrand walked into the light, one hand on the butt of her still-holstered Glock. "I'm just glad you called, Mr. Farrell."

Another figure entered the light -- Elliot Johnson, Bhaava's Director. He looked at Mike and Arnold and said, "I'm disappointed in you boys. Here we've give you every opportunity, and this is how you repay us." Elliot told Richard, "They've both been learning computer skills at Bhaava."

"Mr. Johnson," Mike said, "we were just trying to help."

Chief Hildebrand motioned for Mike to hold out his hands to be cuffed. "This isn't exactly helping," she said. She cuffed Arnold, as well. "Now, the two of you get in that car and behave."

Richard watched in astonishment as the two men headed toward the police cruiser. "Will they actually just get in the car like that?"

"Just like that," the chief said. "I take 'em in all the time. Everyone knows the Gresham brothers. I figured this had to be something they'd concoct."

Elliot said, "They wouldn't really hurt you."

"Hmph! Stand here in the dark with them and tell me that."

Chief Hildebrand said, "I do have to thank you for taking whatever risk there might've been."

"I appreciate that. I'd also appreciate if one of you -- or both of you -- would finally tell me what this is all about."

The chief and Elliot traded glances. Chief Hildebrand said, "You realize he's not going to stop, don't you?"

Elliot lowered his head. "I suppose he isn't."

The chief said, "Let me get these two guys in the pokey. Then we'll all talk."

———

RICHARD AND ALICE CLIMBED THE SMALL RISE THAT LED TO their father's grave. The snow had melted days earlier, soaking the ground just before a cold snap hardened the landscape. "Watch out," Richard said as he took Alice's arm. "It's slippery."

Alice said, "I can't believe you brought us out here on another cold day when it's about to snow. Just to have this conversation in front of Dad."

"I thought we should have this conversation in his presence," Richard said.

"As much of his presence as we have left, anyway."

"I can't believe you're not taking this more seriously."

"You do know about humor covering an inner pain, right?"

They arrived at their father's grave, looked down upon it. Alice knelt and brushed aside a sheath of wilted flowers. She looked up at Richard and said, "So tell me."

"It happened back in 1954. He was headed down to Florida to see Mom. Well, she wasn't 'Mom" yet, of course. Not even his wife yet. Stopped in this little Kentucky town, Plainsville. Had a drink at a bar. That's when he ... " Richard lowered his head, rubbed his face.

Alice squeezed Richard's arm. "You really did find out something tough about Dad, didn't you?"

Richard looked up at his sister. "This guy at the bar, Bill Benson, was drunk. Said a few things to Dad, stranger in town, all that. By all accounts, Dad tried to ignore him, but this Benson guy wouldn't stand for that. Started grappling with Dad, Benson ended up pulling a gun. It went off between them, Benson went down."

"Dead?"

"On the spot."

"Oh, my God. Was Dad arrested?"

"Questioned. Everyone in the bar took up for him. Called it either self-defense or an accident. No charges filed."

"Thank God."

"And apparently Benson was considered the town bully. All the locals hated him. So no one held a grudge against Dad."

"But how did Dad end up financing this -- what' s it called?"

"Bhaava. As you can imagine, that name didn't come about until the sixties. Before that, he started helping out Bill Benson's family. Bastard though he was, he did leave behind a wife and four children. The chief told me how the story's been handed down through the decades. Dad felt guilty. Sent them money each month."

"Even though he wasn't at fault. Yeah, that's how he was. I'm sure he saw it as his responsibility."

Richard continued: "Finally, a few years later, Benson's wife asked him to stop. She'd remarried, didn't even want that reminder of that first husband. She moved away from Plainsville soon after. She's never been back, neither have the children. They'd have kids and grandkids of their own now."

"Don't tell me. Dad wanted to keep helping."

"He did. Went down to Plainsville for a month each year. Set up a soup kitchen. Plainsville may not be that big, but there's always people who need help in any community. Did some good investments, made sure that money kept going to help people in Plainsville and all around."

Alice wiped away tears. "All that good work. And he never wanted us to know?"

"He killed a man. At least that's how he thought of it. Told everyone in Plainsville if they spilled the beans he'd stop the flow of money. They didn't really think he would, but they never wanted to take the chance. Even after he died. It was a secret that weighed so much on our Dad he wanted to make sure it never weighed on us, as well."

"But he took an awful experience and made it into something great."

"I'm with you. Benson's death doesn't weigh on me as much as how Dad reacted uplifts me."

Alice said, "I'm . . . sorry I made you take this on all by yourself. It had to be difficult."

Richard smiled. "Not so much once I got into it. Besides,

I can handle only sitting around drinking beer and watching movies eleven months out of the year."

"Eleven months -- oh, wait you're not -- "

"I sure am. There's that one month a year they're expecting somebody to help them out. Plainsville may look like your typical small town, but it's far beyond what I imagined such a town to be. Especially since it's had that weight lifted off, as well."

SURE THING

"WHAT ELSE CAN WE DO BUT MAKE THE BEST OF THIS, NO matter what happens?" Helen tells her husband Joey, who's had a clean record for eleven years after a long stretch of legal troubles.

Soon, she finds out.

OH, PLEASE GOD, HELEN MORRELL THOUGHT AS SHE HEARD the siren of the Kentucky State Trooper's cruiser begin to wail behind them on Interstate 65. *Don't let Joey do anything stupid*. She glanced at the speedometer: 84 in a 70 mph zone. *Right now the worst that can happen is a speeding ticket.*

She glanced at her husband, whose hands gripped the steering wheel with a quiet fury and whose features revealed a grim determination. "Pull *over*," she told him.

The siren seemed to grow more insistent as the cruiser drew closer. A glance back, and Helen got a good look at the trooper's face and she knew every second Joey didn't pull over, the more likely this whole encounter was to turn out bad; more likely that the trooper would get out of the cruiser with his holster unclipped, with his hand on his Glock, more likely to cast a curious eye at them and the interior of their car.

And Joey *still* wasn't pulling over. "Joey, don't tell me — you're not holding, are you?"

As if that broke a spell, Joey began to pull over to the emergency lane. "Of course not, darlin'," he said. "That trip isn't till later."

"You better be telling the truth."

The car's right-hand tires made a crunching sound against gravel at the edge of the emergency lane as their car came to a stop. They were in a rural area; corn fields seemed to stretch to the horizon on either side of the interstate. The siren made a final descending *whoop* and the cruiser stopped a couple of car lengths behind them.

"Keep your hands on the wheel until he asks for your license, Joey."

"I'll put my hands where I want, honey. This ain't no Gestapo state yet." But Helen noticed Joey's hands didn't budge from the wheel.

Nor did the trooper budge from his cruiser. "What's he doing?" Helen wondered.

Joey said, "Checking our license. They always do that. Don't worry. It's not like the car's stolen or anything."

"He'll know your record, Joey."

"He'll know I've been clean for eleven years. Quit your worrying."

Finally the cruiser's door opened and the trooper got out. After a quick glance at oncoming traffic behind him, he didn't take his eyes off Joey and Helen's car. *And sure enough*, Helen thought, *there's that hand right on his pistol.*

Thankfully, it wasn't until the officer leaned over and

tapped on the driver's side window that Joey hit the control to lower it. "Good morning, officer," he said in a voice Helen found altogether too cloying. "What seems to be the problem?"

From her vantage point in the passenger seat, Helen could only see the lower half of the officer's face; it seemed clean-shaven and square-jawed enough for a recruiting poster. In contrast, she realized Joey must look like a bum. His t-shirt sported gravy stains — the only time Joey put on a shirt with a collar was to work the room at their diner — and his graying hair was disheveled. The officer asked,"Do you know how fast you were going, sir?"

"I guess faster than I thought, officer. Just in a hurry to get home from the grocery."

Helen focused on that hand resting on the Glock, enough that most of the exchange between the trooper and her husband went unheard. Then the trooper pulled out a pad, wrote on it, and made Joey sign for the ticket. As he handed it back to the officer, Joey said, "You've given me such professional service, I'd like a business card, officer."

Oh, no, Joey, just let the man leave.

Even seeing only the lower half of the trooper's face, Helen could tell the request perturbed him. Helen thought, *If Joey's going to pull something, this is the moment, when the trooper takes his hand off the Glock to pull out a card.*

The trooper's right hand continued to rest lightly on his weapon, however, as he pulled a card out of his shirt pocket with his left hand. Joey flashed a smarmy smile. "Thanks, Officer — " He looked down at the card. "Ralph Weston!" Helen knew this trick, too. She snatched the card from Joey's hand before he could tear up the card in the trooper's face. She slid it into a front pocket of her jeans.

The trooper went back to his cruiser. Joey put his

window back up, checked his mirror, and pulled slowly out onto I-65 again. "God *damn* that trooper," he said. That ticket will be over two hundred dollars with court costs!"

"You shouldn't speed."

"Another precinct heard from."

"Are you going to speed on your way to tonight's drug deal?"

"It's just dope. You know the diner hardly makes enough to get by."

"You're seeing that Stu Tippett, aren't you? How's he even afford what you're selling?"

"You smoked enough of it in your day. At least I'm not dealing meth."

Helen turned her gaze away from her husband and toward the rolling corn fields that rushed past at a comfortable 67 mph. "You're right, Joey. You're a saint because you're not dealing meth."

As Joey pulled into their garage, Helen still studiously avoided his gaze, and tried not to listen to his continuing rants about cops and how they were all out to get him.

She got out of the car and strode to its rear as she waited for Joey to pop the trunk. Her lips pressed together as she watched him fumbling with his seat belt and taking his damn time getting the keys from the ignition. She wanted to pound on the trunk to get him to hurry, but knew that would only make things worse.

Finally, he thumbed the button on the remote and the trunk lid gave a dull *thunk* and opened just a couple of inches. Helen lifted the lid and started snatching up plastic grocery bags laden with meat, fresh veggies, trash bags, toilet paper — all the practical needs of their house, which was attached to the rear of their diner.

Actually, *his* diner. Joey's Diner was more than a name, it was a legal fact — he'd never allowed Helen to sign on as a co-owner, saying he didn't want to put that kind of responsibility on her. *More like he wants to keep me in my place*, she thought as she headed to the back door of their house.

Helen and Joey didn't speak as they went through the familiar routine of putting away the food and household goods. Helen found herself listening to the muffled sounds of sizzling burgers, clunking pans, and raised voices from the diner's kitchen, just beyond their living room.

Even on days she wasn't working, those sounds were a constant presence, a constant irritant. *It pays our bills*, Helen conceded to herself. *That and selling dope. But not enough to get us a house separate from the diner*.

As she placed a final head of lettuce into the refrigerator's crisper, Helen kept her voice as even as she could as she asked, "So what time is your other...appointment?"

Joey went to her and grasped her arm with a surprising tenderness. "Don't worry, baby. I've got a big payoff just ahead, a sure thing, and things will be different."

"You'll just waste it on that big game system and HD TV you want."

"That's postponed," Joey said, heading into the living room and plopping down on the couch. "I've got better things to spend the money on."

Helen settled into a chair across from him. "Like what? The sprinkler system in the diner?" Joey had collected nine thousand dollars of insurance money during the winter to repair some frozen pipes in the diner. Instead, Joey had fixed the damage himself, no doubt poorly, and reneged on his promise to her to use the money to fix their broken sprinkler system. She dreaded the next code inspection.

"That's a waste of money. I make everyone be really careful in there. No one's gonna let a fire get out of control."

A sharp, sustained sound of metal clashing against metal punctuated Joey's words and made Helen wince. "You were saying?"

"They drop stuff, Helen! It's not the same as a fire. That sprinkler money is going to better things."

"It was nine thousand dollars — where's it going?"

"Just don't worry yourself. We'll be fine." Joey rose from the couch and opened the door to the short hallway that led to the diner's kitchen. As the opposite door closed, he could hear Joey's booming voice adding to the cacophony within.

HELEN FELL INTO BED EARLY, STILL CLOTHED, ADMITTING SHE just wanted this day to be over. *Joey's gotten better*, Helen thought. But he still wasn't good enough. Sometimes she wondered why she'd stayed with him through a string of arrests for drug deals and petty thefts starting fifteen years earlier.

She was tired of dealing with him, tired of his empty promises, of him skirting the edge of legality. *He even cheats some of his dope clients*, she thought, *either "shorting" them on product or convincing them it was such good "shit" that it was worth paying a premium. Good thing there ain't a one of them very smart.*

At least he ain't hit me in years. I reminded him that if he ever hit me again, he still had to sleep sometime. Then his balls would be mine.

I think he found some respect for me then, she thought, and drifted off to sleep . . .

———

...AND AWAKENED ABRUPTLY WITH JOEY SHAKING HER shoulders. Helen tried to push him off her, but he was telling her, "Get up! We've got to get out of here!"

That's when Helen smelled the smoke. "Oh, no, not —"

"Yes, the restaurant's on fire. Com'on!"

"We've got to grab some things — "

Joey tugged on her arm. "No, we don't — come *on*!"

As they rushed out the rear of their home, Helen saw a crimson glow washing over Joey's back. She turned, and her heart dropped at the sight of the flames dancing into dark skies. The wind shifted the smoke around toward them and Helen covered her mouth as she coughed. Sirens screamed from several blocks away, growing louder.

Joey opened his arms toward her. She stepped into them and they embraced. He said quietly, his mouth against her ear, "I could never stand to lose you, baby. Never."

———

THE FIRST FAINT GLOW SIGNALING DAWN FADED INTO HELEN'S awareness as she stood watching the firefighters put out hot spots in the rubble of Joey's Diner. The fire had gotten such a head start on the small volunteer department that they'd only managed to contain the fire, not keep it from destroying the building. A few wooden beams stuck up from the wreckage, their silhouette against the red skies to the east looking like the ribs of a skeleton.

Joey had fetched a blanket for her somewhere and in the

morning chill she shrugged her shoulders to pull it tighter around herself. *At least they saved the house*, she thought as she watched county sheriff's officers putting up the yellow crime scene tape around the site.

All the neighbors who had gathered around to gawk at their misfortune were gone now, no doubt sleeping soundly in their nice safe beds. Hardly a one had actually come up to her to profess sympathy or ask what they could do for her.

She started as a hand clamped down on her shoulder. Joey. "Sorry if I scared ya, babe. I talked to Stu Tippett. He'll put us up for a few days, until we can get back in the house."

"What's left of it."

"The living room's got some smoke damage. That's about it."

"But the diner's gone."

"We'll rebuild. Better than ever."

"How will we pay for it?"

"You let me worry about that."

Right, Helen thought. *As if I won't be worrying enough for both of us.* "How long until we can come back?"

"The arson investigation could take a day or so, they said."

"*Arson*? What makes them think — "

"Don't worry, honey. That's standard. Besides, the county's got one arson investigator, name of Glenn Raines, and I hear he doesn't know a match from a milkshake."

"He lives just down the street, doesn't he? I hope he's not one of your customers."

"Only a couple of times at the restaurant, dearie. He'll call it an accident within a day, and be done with it."

"With your record, you'll have to be under suspicion."

"How many times do I hafta tell ya, darlin'? My *clean* record of eleven years." He took her hand and looked her in the eyes, exhibiting an affection she hadn't seen in too long a time.

Before she gave herself a chance to think, Helen cupped Joey's face with her hand and gave him a lingering kiss. "You're right. What else can we do but make the best of this, no matter what happens?"

HELEN FOUND THAT STU TIPPETT WASN'T THE LOW-LIFE SHE'D expected, though his home was sparsely furnished and, if messy, at least not dirty.

A tall, slender, bearded man in his mid-thirties, Stu was an EMT with the county. As he showed Helen and Joey the spare bedroom where they could stay, he wouldn't look Helen in the eye at first. Helen was unpacking a small suitcase when Joey went into the hall bathroom to wash up. It was only then that Stu told her, in a small voice, "I hope you don't think bad of me because I use your husband's...services."

Helen paused in her unpacking. "That's...not for me to say."

"I'm divorced. Work a high-stress job. It relaxes me."

Helen found herself smiling. "I have no reason to be holier-than-thou. I appreciate you taking us in."

"Joey was telling me about the arson investigation. It really is routine."

"I know."

"And Glenn Raines is an idiot. It's too bad. If he was smarter, he could advance up the ranks and make more money. He wants to send his son to trade school. But he can't afford it."

"That's too bad. I can't believe someone that incompetent even gets to keep the job he has."

"He knows people. There's a lot of corruption in this county. So they don't fire him, even though he could find a trail of gasoline leading to an empty gas can and rule the fire accidental."

"So when it really *is* accidental..."

"If it is, you shouldn't have a problem."

As Stu excused himself and left, Helen's breath quickened and she fought to suppress her growing concern.

JOEY SHOOK HELEN AWAKE, AND SHE IMMEDIATELY FLASHED back to the night of the fire. She sat up in panic, then realized she was in Stu's spare bedroom. Joey told her, "It's OK. Glenn Raines is here."

Helen rubbed her face to wipe away the final vestiges of sleep. "The...arson guy?"

"I think he's got good news. He came right here to see us even though he usually works nights."

"Lemme get some decent clothes on and we'll go see."

As Helen dressed, she noticed the time — ten in the morning. Stu would already have gone to work. Sure enough, when she went out to the living room, only Joey and Raines were there, sitting in a couple of Stu's ragged chairs across from one another.

Raines was a round-faced man in his mid-thirties, prematurely balding. His handshake as he rose to greet her was perfunctory. "I have good news for you, Mrs. Morrell. I've ruled the fire in your diner an accident."

Helen cast her previous worries aside and embraced Joey. "Oh, that's great! But what caused it?"

Raines spread his hands and tilted his head as if to say it didn't matter. "Probably something electrical. But definitely not an arson."

Joey told Helen, "Which is great news for us — we can collect on our insurance — three million dollars!"

Helen almost gasped, and pressed her lips together before they could form the phrase "big payoff." Instead, she asked Raines, "When can we go back into the house?"

"Any time. It's not exactly by the book to let you back in — the part of the diner backed up against the living room isn't that stable. But as long as you stay out of the front part of the house, you should be fine."

"I don't care how unstable any of it is. I just want to be back in our house."

Joey said, "Then let's go, baby!"

HELEN AND JOEY PACKED THEIR STUFF, LEFT STU A NOTE thanking them for taking them in, and piled into their car and headed home. They hadn't been back there since the morning of the fire, and Helen's heart ached as she and Joey pulled up to the charred and collapsed remnants of the diner. The crime scene tape was gone, but Joey had paid to have a chain link fence raised around the remnants of the diner. "Can't have just anybody walking around in there," he said.

As Helen got out of the car, she recalled all the hard work that had gone into building a customer base from scratch — the long hours, the wrangling for good deals with food vendors and delivery services, Joey in back hectoring his young and inexperienced workers, her carrying heavy trays of food out to customers alternately grateful and demanding.

As she stood there, Joey put an arm around her shoulders. "It'll be all right soon, babe."

"If this insurance deal comes through..."

"*When*, babe. It's a sure thing."

"Yeah. We'll make a bigger place — state-of-the-art kitchen, nicer seats for the customers, everything we always wanted. And a separate house, so we can live without hearing pans dropping and people yelling."

"Helen, when that deal comes through, we can sit and rock on our new front porch and tell everyone who passes by to go straight to hell."

Helen grinned. "That's a heck of a goal in life."

"It's the *only* one, baby. I know I haven't always been the best husband. I'm here to make it up to you." Joey slipped his arm from her shoulders and walked toward the back of the structure, the mostly undamaged part that was still, for now, their home.

Everything's going to change, Helen thought. *The question is, how, and — is it something we deserve?*

———

THE NEXT MORNING, JOEY TOOK THE CAR DOWNTOWN, SAYING it was to talk to a lawyer about their insurance settlement, to see if the process could be sped up. This was the first Helen had heard of this unnamed lawyer, and she suspected he was actually meeting up with a drug customer. *Any money he comes back with, he'll say it's an "advance" on our settlement. But I know better.*

And I think Stu had something to do with this. Which means

I need to talk to Glenn Raines, and see if he knows more than he's letting on.

Raines lived just down the street from her and Joey, and Helen remembered he usually worked nights. But a resurgent fear made Helen hesitate at the front door of Raines' unassuming home; if you'd asked her why she came here, she would've attributed it to a whim, perhaps, or wanting to make sure that Joey really had changed, that they would be able to enjoy their upcoming insurance settlement with a clear conscience.

In for a little, in for a lot, she thought, and rang the doorbell. She waited a long moment, and was undecided whether to ring the bell again or try to knock really loud when she heard movement just beyond the front door. An instant later it opened, tentatively, and a teenager looking to be about seventeen or eighteen, presumably Bobby Raines, stood before Helen. He didn't say anything.

Helen pushed on. "Hi. Is your dad home?"

"He's at work."

"Oh. I thought he worked nights."

"Usually. But someone got sick."

"Well...heck. Maybe I'll try back later."

"OK," the teen said, and, perhaps remembering a procedure he'd skipped, asked Helen, "Who should I say called?"

"Helen Morrell. I'm — "

"You're Mr. Morrell's wife!"

"Yes, I — "

"Do you wanna com'on in? Can I give you a glass of tea or something?"

"No, really, I —

"Hey, I just wanted to thank you and Mr. Morrell."

Helen had to pause a moment before asking, "Thank us?"

"For the money so I can go to trade school. He's supposed to give us the next installment soon." Then Bobby slapped his hand across his mouth. "Oops! That was supposed to be a secret, wasn't it?"

Helen fought through rising fury to keep her voice even and calm as she told Bobby, "Don't worry about it. That'll be *our* secret."

HELEN MANAGED TO HOLD THINGS TOGETHER UNTIL SHE walked home, then went into the bedroom and pounded out her frustrations against a mound of pillows as tears flowed freely down her cheeks. *Installments*, she thought. *It wasn't Stu who was involved at all, it was Glenn. And he didn't set the fire — he covered it up. The nine thousand dollars went to him. And no doubt he's getting part of our three million.*

Which means Joey set fire to our own diner. Risked losing our home, as well. And he managed to get me out of the house, but what if he'd miscalculated?

Exhausted, Helen let herself drop face-down onto the bed. After a few moments, tears dried up, she rose from the bed and started searching the laundry basket for the jeans she'd worn the day she and Joey had been pulled over for speeding.

HELEN WAS AMAZED AT THE QUICK RESPONSE TO HER PHONE call. By the time Joey returned, crime scene tape was being put up again, not by sheriff's deputies, but by state troopers.

Joey skidded the car to a stop and got out, slamming the door and heading straight for Helen. "What the hell is going on here?" he demanded, and started to reach for Helen's arm.

A uniformed arm came between them. The trooper asked Joey, "Remember me, Mr. Morrell?"

Joey sputtered and took a step back. "Wait a minute — you're — "

"Officer Ralph Weston. I gave you my card."

"I *paid* that ticket. What the hell does — "

"This isn't about the ticket, sir. This is about the diner. I obtained a court order allowing us to look into allegations of improprieties involving this property — and an insurance claim."

Helen watched as Joey managed to set aside his anger and appear to become reasonable. "Really, Officer Weston, this has already been investigated."

"We're talking to Glenn Raines about the nature of his investigation. It appears he's cooperating."

"But he didn't find anything!"

"Our own arson investigators should be here within a day or two. We'll see if they find something he...overlooked." Helen felt a pang of regret for Bobby Raines, who would lose his dad for however many years Glenn was sentenced to prison, and wouldn't get to go to trade school.

Joey turned toward Helen. "If I go to jail, you're going, too! We were in this diner together, you know."

"Actually, Joey, I wasn't. Everything's in your name, remember? Any payoff went to you alone."

"What are you going to do? We had a sure thing, here."

Helen looked Joey in the eye. "I guess I'll have to get a job, won't I? Shouldn't be hard, with all my experience in the diner business. And my clean record."

Officer Weston said, "Time to move along now, Mr. Morrell. We'd like to take you to the post to answer some questions."

As Officer Weston marched Joey toward his cruiser, he stopped and turned toward Helen again. "Oh, Mrs. Weston, as you can imagine, we'll need to you come in at some point and make a detailed statement."

Helen nodded to Weston, then looked at Joey with a wistfulness for what might have been if he'd been a different man.

"Sure thing," she said.

SAFE HOUSE

A MOTHER'S LOVE CAN LEAD HER TO MAKE A DESPERATE choice . . . .

———

DETECTIVE EDWARD GALVAN NODDED AT THE UNIFORMS standing outside Patty Keller's house and took the rough concrete steps toward the front door two at a time, hope mixing with concern. *A mother who takes her child away from an abusive husband and goes missing for the better part of a year doesn't just appear out of nowhere one night*, he thought. *And if she does, she doesn't immediately disappear again. It doesn't make sense.*

An image of his own beloved family flashed unbidden into his mind, but he pushed it aside — this was work time, and thoughts of his wife Debbie and children Ethan and Kathy had to wait.

It was a warm night; the inner wooden door leading into Keller's living room stood open. Galvan knocked lightly on the outer screen door while holding his shield so she could see it. Keller, who was sitting on a couch next to a thin blonde girl of ten or eleven, waved him in.

Keller put an arm around the child's shoulders and squeezed. Then she stood, extending her hand toward Galvan. The top of her head barely came up to his chin. She had wide eyes and a model's cheekbones, and thick shoulder-length hair.

"Patty Keller."

"Detective Edward Galvan."

"I want to thank the officers outside for understanding, and waiting outside." She indicated the girl and spoke quietly. "Heather's become so used to avoiding the police — she sees a police car or anyone in a uniform and she gets so scared. But when Rebecca dropped her off and just told off again, I had to call you."

Galvan glanced over at the girl, who had curled up into one corner of the couch, legs folded beneath her, arms hugging herself. He kept his own voice low. "You haven't had any contact with Heather's father?"

Keller shook her head. "The bastard. Name's Douglas. He beat Rebecca, sometimes right in front of Heather. She'd leave him, then he'd promise to be better and she'd go back to him. Then he'd beat her again. You know the pattern."

"It's a tough one to break for some women."

"Well, finally Rebecca had enough. The courts were moving too slowly. She took Heather and left. Didn't even tell me where she was going."

"Did you have any contact with her at all this past year?" Galvan saw Keller hesitate, quickly said, "You're not going to get in trouble if you have. I just need to know whatever you can tell me about what's been going on."

Keller took a deep breath. "I talked to her a couple times

on the phone. She said she was on cheap phones that she'd throw away afterwards — "

"Burner phones, they call them."

"Yes, that's it. Not that I'd know how to trace her, or even want to. She just let me know she was OK, and so was Heather."

"Did she ask for money or any other kind of assistance?"

"No, never."

"And tonight she just showed up without any warning."

"Just like that."

Galvan asked, "When she left here, how'd she act toward Heather?"

"What do you mean?"

"Did she make it a casual goodbye, or like she wouldn't be seeing her for awhile?"

"Well, I guess I *did* notice that. She gave Heather a long hug, told her to be good for me, then a couple kisses on the cheek and another long hug."

"Did she say where she was going?"

"No. But I can guess."

"Me, too. Where's her husband live?"

"Not five blocks away, right here in the Highlands. Gives me the creeps that he's so close."

"I have the address," Galvan said as he headed for the door. "I'm going right there."

GALVAN RADIOED DISPATCH AND REQUESTED A UNIFORMED unit to head toward Douglas Stoker's home, but when he heard their ETA he realized he'd get there first. *Most likely,* he thought, *I'm being melodramatic and once I get there, I'll find*

Douglas Stoker sitting and watching TV, wondering what all the commotion is about.

Then dispatch called him back. "We've had a report of shots fired at that location you gave us," the dispatcher said. "I've told the uniforms to step it up, respond Code Three." That meant lights and sirens.

"Ten-four, dispatch," Galvan said. "I'm coming up on the scene now."

Galvan pulled up in front of Douglas Stoker's two-story frame home. As he got out of the car, he saw a mirror image of the scene at Patty Keller's house — inner front door ajar, outer screen door closed. Bright lights inside the living room. A woman sitting on a couch, head down, hands folded in front of her. No visible weapon.

No sign of Douglas Stoker.

A police cruiser's siren wailed from about a block away.

Even from the street, Galvan could tell this woman had the same wide eyes and prominent cheekbones as Patty Keller, and similar thick shoulder-length hair. *Some dominant genes in this family*, he thought. *That* has *to be Rebecca Stoker.*

The police cruiser pulled up behind him. He told the uniforms, a man and a woman, "We're going to talk to that woman sitting on the couch. I don't know whether she's a victim or a possible suspect. We're also keeping an eye out for her husband."

The female uniform asked, "Is he a victim or a suspect?"

"We don't know yet. Let's go."

Galvan pulled his Glock and started up the sidewalk toward Douglas Stoker's house. As he drew close to the doorway, Rebecca Stoker looked up at him for an instant, then lowered her head again.

Keeping his firearm at his side, Galvan eased the screen

door open. "You might as well come on in," Rebecca Stoker said. "It's over."

On the other side of the living room, a man's body was lying on its back. Galvan could see at least two bullet wounds in his chest. He hadn't even bled out that much.

Galvan told the male officer, "Get EMS here." That officer nodded and headed back toward the cruiser. The female officer stayed by the doorway.

"It's no use," Rebecca Stoker said. "He's gone."

"Where's the gun?" Galvan asked her.

She pointed toward a far corner of the room. "Over there. Once I did it, I didn't want it near me anymore."

"I have to read you your rights."

"My *rights*? That's a joke. I had the right to be beaten. I had the right to live in fear for years at a time."

Galvan put away his Glock. "I have to ask you to stand up."

Rebecca Stoker stood. "I was out of time," she said. "I had to give Heather a decent life, a regular life."

"A regular life would've been one where her mother isn't in prison."

"I won't make it to prison," Rebecca Stoker said, and grabbed the top of her hair and pulled it off.

A wig! She dropped it to the floor and said, "I have ovarian cancer. By the time I knew I was getting sick, I was already in hiding with Heather. A few months ago I came out of hiding to be treated — they got as far as one round of chemo before telling me we'd found it too late. I just had months to live."

Galvan wasn't sure how to respond at first. Finally, he said, "I'm sorry."

Rebecca Stoker said, "So, you see, I didn't have a lot of time left. I kept my head shaved to remind me of what I was facing. I had to make sure I could make a good life for Heather. I knew giving her over to Patty would work out — they adore one another."

She fought back tears. "But Douglas — damn him! How could I protect her from him?"

Galvan said, "So you came here."

Rebecca Stoker indicated the still body on the floor. "And did that."

Galvan could just make out the wailing siren of the EMS wagon. He pulled out his cuffs. "I have to ask you to turn around."

She did, and Galvan placed the cuffs around her wrists. He didn't make them as tight as he could have.

"It was all I could do," Rebecca Stoker said. "Don't you see? Heather deserves a safe house to live in. That's all I wanted for her, was a safe house."

"You did that, Rebecca. You surely did."

The EMS med-techs got out of the ambulance and headed toward the house. Once they passed Galvan on what would be a futile mission to save Douglas Stoker, he waved the female uniformed officer over. She took Rebecca Stoker's arm and led her toward the police cruiser, as Galvan allowed himself a moment to think of Debbie and Ethan and Kathy, and how he intended to sweep each of them up in his arms once he got home, and wished he could never let them out of his sight again.

FOR LAUREN

ANOTHER PARENT, AND ANOTHER SET OF DESPERATE CHOICES.

———

THE TOUGHEST PART ABOUT PLANNING A NEW SERIES OF burglaries was putting aside concern over my daughter. Casing a new neighborhood takes a lot of concentration — everyone knows you should make sure to cancel the newspaper and the mail when you go on vacay, but not everyone does it.

My job's to look for those houses.

But I don't just stay passive, not by any means. I tell the owners of a local pizza place how much I love their place, and offer to stick some flyers into front doors in "my" neighborhood. They look at you funny, but I know I'll never see them again, because I never pick the same pizza joint twice. Place the flyers along a couple blocks of a particular street, then come back three or four days later and see them still flapping in the breeze at a couple homes, and bingo! No one's home, I've got new targets, each worth a few hundred dollars here or there if I make a good haul.

It also helps to be nosy, but you've got to have a plan — I keep a notepad in my pickup, and make sure to carry it around as I look into windows or check out what's sitting around on a backyard deck. What do you mean, what am I doing here? I'm the meter reader. Oh, the meter's on the other side of the house? So sorry.

Skip that one. Can't have the homeowner remembering me — yes, officer, there was that one guy said he was a meter reader. Tall, pale, looked like he could use a nap.

He'd be right about that. Anyway, casing homes is how I spend most of my days and many of my nights, while my daughter Lauren stays in a daycare that helps special kids like her, or sometimes with my sister Karen in her apartment. Karen, by the way, must be a saint to put up with this.

By "this," I don't mean Lauren — Karen finds her to be a joy — I mean me.

I know Karen and I have it pretty lucky — Lauren's autism isn't as difficult to deal with as it is for a lot of parents. Here in Louisville, Kentucky, we've got plenty of resources — both medical ones and things like support groups — to make things easier.

And I know the drill — keep a tight schedule for schools, meals, therapy, bedtime. Praise goes a lot farther than criticism, especially when your child's learning something new. Lauren's seven, and it's been a long time since she's had a major meltdown in school or at a restaurant.

Most of the credit goes to her, of course, but I'm not ashamed to take a lot of it for myself. I just wish Christy, her mother, could've seen how she's improving. It's a bitch for the love of your life to die of cancer at age 35.

So my days are spent looking for targets. Karen thinks I'm a professional gardener. I did some of that right after my construction job went south. Tough economy. Didn't help that I wasn't my own best friend. Drank too much, got into arguments when a contractor didn't want to hire me right away. Quit drinking — mostly — but the word had gotten around. No one wants to work with a hothead twenty stories up.

But that didn't pay enough. Lauren's therapy is expensive. I've put off repairs to the pickup and the house, skipped meals, and even borrowed from Karen.

So here I am, having to put thoughts of Lauren aside as I drive through this well-manicured neighborhood, looking for piles of newspapers, overflowing mailboxes, and front doors with "my" pizza flyers sticking out of them.

The worst part of it all is, even though I tell myself I'm just doing this until I find a "real" job, and only so I can pay for Lauren's care, I think, deep in my heart, I'm actually starting to like it.

———

FOR THE FIRST FEW MONTHS, THINGS WORKED OUT JUST THE way my research on the web said they would. Even burglars take pride in their job — they share their best practices, they tell "war stories" about close calls or how they talked their way out of a bad situation where it turned out the homeowner was present after all.

It happens, despite taking all the best precautions. I concentrated my efforts in the Clifton and Crescent Hill parts of town, since I grew up in the area and I'm familiar with its neighborhoods and all the side streets and back alleys.

At least I've managed to avoid the chump mistakes, so far. Especially since I've had to skip some truck repairs, I make sure to check all my lights so I know they're working properly, and I'm always careful never to commit a traffic violation. And I keep my drivers license and plate current. More burglars get caught with stolen stuff in their vehicles on a traffic stop than at the scene of the crime.

You gotta be careful approaching a home, too. Untouched pizza flyers don't always tell the whole story. Knock on the door just to make sure no one's home, and your eyes grow wide when the door opens and a surly guy in a soiled robe who hasn't shaved in three days answers, "Whadda ya want?"

Then you hand him the flyer, explain you're following up to see why he hasn't used it, he mumbles something about how his garage is in the back and he never uses the front door and never saw the damn thing.

You thank him and leave without trying to seem as if you're in a hurry, the whole time bitching at yourself because that guy's big screen TV looked mighty fine from the street.

One day, though, I found myself in a situation I'd never considered. At least, I'd never thought I'd be outfoxed by a competitor.

Everything seemed right. Papers piled up in the driveway. Mailbox bulging. Pizza flyer untouched. Knock on the front door — no answer. So I backed the pickup into the driveway until it was even with the rear of the house. This was the day after the unshaven robe guy and I was determined to snag a big screen TV.

I had everything planned out. I'd use one of those safety

hammers that you use to bust your window when you've driven your car into the river. I'd break the glass in the home's rear door's window. Sure, it makes some noise, but you just have to make sure to keep things quiet after that. Most of the time, anyone who lives next door will perk up at that one loud noise, but if she doesn't hear another, it's usually back to her soap. Wait a minute, most of the soaps are dead — maybe THE VIEW or THE CHEW or whatever the hell is on nowadays.

So I had my gloves on, the hammer out and ready to go. I made my way to the back door —

And its window was already broken.

The hell? I thought, and I admit I stood there dumbfounded for a couple seconds. I won't tell you how fast my heart was racing — I was afraid of coming in on somebody in the middle of their own job. And even though I'm a burly guy — I was about to manhandle a big screen TV out the door on my own, remember — I know there's always someone bigger around.

But curiosity got the better of me. I eased the door open. It entered directly onto the family room, which was one reason I picked this house.

I eased myself past a musty-looking couch that had seen better days. One cushion was littered with popcorn kernels, one couch arm had a bowling shirt lying upon it, black down the middle and blue down the sides, with the team name on the left breast: Lucky Strikes. *Great*, I thought. *Very original*.

On the other side of the couch, the TV was gone, along with the Blu-ray player and the sweet sound system. A nest of wires, their various branches reaching upward like mummified fingers, were the only evidence of their existence, that and several dust bunnies.

"Damn," I found myself saying out loud, and turned and high-tailed it out of there. It would be bad enough to get caught committing my own crime, but going to jail for someone else's? No thank you.

It's NOT YOUR FAULT, I TOLD MYSELF AS I EASED THE PICKUP out of that neighborhood, keeping things calm, *It's all total coincidence that someone got there ahead of you.*

But who was that someone? And wait — could it really be coincidence? Was someone following behind me, and while I was casing "my" homes, were *they* casing *me*?

Damn, I thought, *this is too spooky. I might want to set this whole burglary thing aside for awhile.*

But I knew I couldn't. I needed the money. *Lauren* needed the money, and she was more important than anything to me.

You gotta get right back on that horse, I thought, and, being careful to pull to a complete stop at every intersection and to use my signals properly, I headed toward a backup target in a nearby neighborhood.

I should'a led that hypothetical horse right back into the barn.

JUST A COUPLE BLOCKS OVER, I'D GOTTEN LUCKY WHILE driving past another home earlier in the week, or so I thought. I'd gotten a glimpse at what looked like an affluent couple who lived there, and though I couldn't get a good look at anything specific, I just knew there had to be some jewelry there, maybe some stashes of cash. The high quality of their landscaping and above-ground pool suggested that.

What made the home especially appealing — the front door featured decorative glass — very pretty, all different shades of blue and green. But the installer for the alarm company had been stupid, and placed the control pad for the alarm where anyone could see it by peeking through the pretty glass.

My plan was simple — knock at the front door as usual, and if there wasn't a response, check to see if the alarm was off. If it was, I'd go around back and break into the rear door or a window and take a look around as quickly as possible.

I'd check the bedrooms — that's where you usually find the valuables or stashes of money. If this couple was smarter than most, and I came up short there, then I'd look under the mattresses, inside medicine cabinets, or behind pictures or even inside freezers. Most people fit into familiar patterns.

So — pull up, get out of the pickup, head to the front door. Knock. No response. I peer in through the glass — there you go, the alarm isn't set.

By mere whim, I take hold of the doorknob and twist — the door opens! That was easy! Never mind the back door, now. The first glance inside is optimistic — nice furniture, all recent stuff, pretty expensive, the home spotless.

But from a darkened corner of the room — a voice rings out, that of an elderly woman, a bit shaky but still booming out strong. "Roger — is that you? Why did you knock?"

My eyes try to pierce the darkness. I can just make out a sitting form in a rocking chair. She isn't rocking, and I just make out something in her hands. A cane, perhaps? But no, her cane's next to her, and I can see that's it's a cane for the blind, white and red-tipped.

My first thought is, *At least she can't see me, identify me.* I start forward, intending to rush into the next room, snatch what I can before this old and slow woman could catch up, and head out the back door.

But the woman speaks again before I can take a step: "Whoever you are, I may be blind, but I can hear just fine, and unless you tell me the password, and say it in my son's voice, I'm going to shoot."

Password? *Shoot*? I spin around, meaning to dash back out the front door, but the shotgun blast comes before I can get there. I feel the sting of several wounds against my back, and shut my eyes tightly against flying shards of that very pretty decorative glass.

Then it's out the door, into the truck, and get the key into the ignition. Turn the key —

And the truck shudders and fails.

Got to make those repairs, I think as I glance over to the house, fearing I'll see that old woman headed toward me, shotgun at the ready to finish the job she started. But she isn't there, and I make myself turn the key a little less forcefully this time.

The truck's engine turns over, and I rabbit out of there, and for once I don't give a damn about traffic violations. All that matters when I get to that first stop sign is that no one's coming the other direction — I blow through it as if it never existed.

———

I DROVE HOME IN A DAZE — YOU KNOW HOW IT FEELS WHEN your car — or in my case, pickup — "just knows the way?" That's how I reacted. I was barely aware of pulling into my own driveway, going into my house the back way, entering directly into my kitchen, and removing my shirt off as I headed toward the bathroom. As I examined the shirt, I decided the old lady must've been firing birdshot rather than anything designed for a larger target — like a human — and didn't have very good aim, to boot. As it was, she only hit me in four or five places, and those pellets had barely pierced my shirt. I could make out only a couple streaks of blood in the fabric. *Thank goodness for that*, I thought. *That means I probably didn't leave any blood spatter behind as evidence.*

I didn't waste any time, though. I took a quick shower, reasoning that would be the quickest way to clean my wounds. As I dried off my back, I checked my towel for blood, didn't see any. *I was lucky*, I thought. *Although, if I was that lucky, I wouldn't have been shot in the first place.*

As I dressed, I put on a new shirt, cut the old one up into rags, placed it into a plastic grocery bag, and took a walk. When I reached the convenience mart down the street, I went around back and stashed the bag into the store's dumpster. I was tempted to stop in to grab some beer to take home, but I didn't want to be picked up on the store's surveillance system in case anyone had reason to try to track my whereabouts later. Better safe than sorry.

That night on the news, all four local stations had stories on the old lady who shot up her own front door. I know because I kept flipping back and forth between channels, praying that no one had a clue who she'd shot at.

No one did. My paranoid fear that one of the news reporters on the scene would call out my name, Phillip McAllister, and that the cops would be knocking on my door in the next instant, turned out to be unfounded. At least for now.

In fact, even though the affluent looking couple had clammed up (the old woman was the husband's mother), the official police spokesman, a soft-spoken man in plainclothes, seemed to imply that maybe the old lady had just shot at a random noise, and there was never anyone there. I'm grateful I'd never said a word while inside the house, and even managed to shut the door behind me even as I was dodging birdshot.

But then, during one report, came the big surprise — it seemed that despite the doubt cast upon the shotgun granny, there *had* been a series of burglaries in the area recently — as many as five or six, the reporter said.

But I haven't done more than a couple over that way, I thought. *Someone else must be —*

Dammit! It must be whoever stole that TV before I got there. Same neighborhood, around the same time of day.

I've got to keep an eye out — I don't want to find myself getting caught because I've stumbled upon something else this guy's done.

———

THE NEXT COUPLE OF DAYS, THOUGH, THE HORSE *WOULD* STAY in the barn. I stuck close to home, bringing Lauren home early from daycare (grateful that it was within walking distance) and spending as much time as I could with her, preferring the extra time with her even with the risk a change in routine might bring. I reveled in these extra hours with her, always marveling at how pretty she was (and how glad I was she took after Christie instead of me), and how lucky I was to have her despite the difficulties her autism brought.

And, Lord forgive me, I was grateful that she was a girl. Autism is four times more common in boys than girls, so not as much is known about how to deal with autistic girls. But it turns out girls with autism are much more social than boys.

I'd sit on the living room floor and read a Harry Potter book to Lauren, and she'd be enthralled for the better part of half an hour before demanding we do something else. That "something else" could be something as mundane as playing with Barbies. I'd fill the house with them if I could, because they let Lauren be a model, a businesswoman, a nurse, an astronaut, all in one day, and I was glad to see her creating a fantasy life for herself that one day, I hoped, would help her create a real, adult life.

But for now, some things were cast in stone. Dinner precisely at 6:00. Bath right after. Storytime at 8:00, bed at 8:30.

Just another day in the normal life of a normal burglar.

As grateful as I was for these couple of days with Lauren, I knew I had my own routine to stick to. Her therapy doesn't pay for itself. I had to get back on the street, and I had to do it soon.

———

WHAT DID I TELL MYSELF BEFORE? *YOU GOTTA GET RIGHT BACK on that horse.*

Somehow I'd given myself temporary amnesia about how that had worked out just days before. I took precautions, though. I had several potential targets I'd already checked out the week before. I made myself be methodical and check them all out again before settling on one.

There's a danger in that, of course. The more times you drive through a neighborhood, the more likely someone will spot you and wonder what you're doing there. Of course, they're also likely just to assume you're someone who moved in down the street that they haven't met yet.

Not that people know the folks down the street these days, anyway.

I was still determined to grab a big screen TV, and after spending much of the morning checking out the various homes I'd scouted before, I picked my target. It had just the TV I wanted — a 51-incher, just big enough to satisfy the average viewer, but not so big I couldn't snatch it myself.

In part, I was drawn to the challenge — covering the screen with blankets and manhandling the dang thing all by myself down some steps and lifting it into my pickup. Tough, dangerous work, but also exciting, and I was looking forward to it.

I'm starting to like this a little too much, I thought. *This is just supposed to be a job.*

But it's not. Not as long as I love Lauren. So — back on the horse.

YOU KNOW THE DRILL BY NOW. VISUAL INSPECTION FROM outside. This was an older neighborhood, and this home and many others in the area were "shotgun" houses — so called because the layout of the rooms extended straight back from the street. In other words, you could shoot a shotgun from the front of the house to the back unimpeded.

"Shotgun," though, was the last word I wanted to think of just then.

Damn if there wasn't one of my ubiquitous pizza flyers still hanging from the front doorknob. Knock on the door. No one answered. I grasped the doorknob and tried to give it a turn, and was actually grateful that it didn't budge. If you can't open the door, it doesn't matter whether there's a shotgun-wielding granny behind it.

So I backed the truck up into the driveway. The garage was in back of the house, which was another reason to pick this target — less chance of being seen bringing the TV out the back than in front.

I got out of the truck, pulled the blankets from out of the bed, and laid them down next to the back door. Got out the safety hammer, looked around, didn't see or hear anyone nearby, and tapped out the glass square of the back door's window nearest to the inside doorknob. Reached in with one gloved hand (no fingerprints, no worries about cutting myself on shattered glass), turned the knob. Eased the door open, grabbed my blankets, and went inside.

Still no grandmas with shotguns. But I was painfully aware of the creaking sound I generated with each step across the bare wooden floorboards of the house. I went through the rear laundry room first, then the kitchen, then a bedroom.

I knew the TV was in the next room, a second bedroom that had been converted into a family room — it had easily been visible through a side window. Given my recent luck (or lack of same), I halfway expected to enter this room and find this TV missing like the earlier one.

But I was wrong! There it was, in all its glory. *Finally*, I thought. It was an expensive model, and certainly it could pick up a few hundred dollars for me, but I'd been so long getting to this point that I had to wonder whether I would be making a good hourly rate by the time I got paid.

I took another creaking step forward —

And saw the body.

Shit, was my first thought, as I looked more closely at the still form of the man. He was lying on his back — he looked to be in his early sixties. Blood had pooled beneath his head. A gold-colored trophy depicting a bowling ball smashing into pins was lying beside him. Its base was bloody.

My instinct was to bolt — what if the police were on the way? I had no desire to be a part of that cliched movie twist where someone who's innocent — or at least as innocent as a burglar gets — is caught at the scene of the crime and has to exonerate himself.

But I couldn't make myself leave just yet. Some good-guy part of me that wondered if this man could still be alive made me kneel down and give him a closer look.

The victim's eyes were open, but obviously unseeing. I waved my hand in front of his eyes to make sure — no reaction. I snapped my fingers next to his ears — again, no response.

He didn't seem to be breathing — I couldn't see his chest move. I pulled off a glove and let the back of my hand hover over his nose and mouth. I felt no breath of life there. I pressed the back of my hand against the man's face. Paradoxically, the instant I touched warm skin, I felt a chill go through me.

I gave a frustrated sigh. I was 90 percent sure this was a dead man. I also knew what I had to do, just in case I was wrong. A quick look around the room, and thank goodness, I saw a landline. I put my glove back on and dialed 911.

In an instant I heard, "*911, what's the nature of your emergency?*"

"I'm at 2172 Crestwood Way, and there's a dead body in the family room."

"Sir, are you a relative? What is — "

I hung up. I'd given them the address, and I knew the 911 system would have picked it up from caller ID, anyway.

I had to get the hell out of here.

But the chill I'd gotten from touching this poor man's still-warm body lingered. My next thought was, *Is my competitor — or whoever did this — still in the house?*

This home was built on a single level. The only room I hadn't been in was the living room, closest to the street. I made myself back away from the body and peeked around the corner.

A fist smacked into the side of my head. In that moment of decision — fight or flight — I went with *fight*, and shoved myself closer to my assailant, hoping to gain some advantage.

A moment of grappling, and I took another blow to the head. As I fell to the floor, I caught a glimpse of a young man heading for the front door. Blonde shoulder-length hair, long sideburns, earring in the left ear. As he opened the door, sunlight pierced the dark living room and I held up my hand against the glare. The guy, just a kid, really, was silhouetted against the sunlight for that instant and I couldn't make out more details. Then he bolted, but before he disappeared, damn if I didn't see that he was wearing a "Lucky Strikes" bowling shirt like the one I'd seen in the home where most likely this same guy had stolen a TV ahead of me. Then the door slammed shut and he was gone.

I needed to be gone, too. I went out the back, hopped into my truck, and tore out of the driveway. It wasn't until I was a couple blocks away that I began to hear sirens in the distance. Heart pounding, face bleeding, I made myself slow down. I caught a glimpse in my rear-view mirror of the first couple police units as they turned down Crestwood Way, paying me no notice.

THIS TIME MY INJURIES HURT A LOT MORE, AND WERE A LOT more visible. I was glad I was picking up Lauren from daycare that afternoon and not from Karen's apartment — a couple of the workers at the daycare looked askance at my bruised face as I fetched my daughter, but Karen would've spoken up and had a few questions for me.

As for Lauren, apparently my new appearance wasn't enough of a change to make much of an impression. As I placed her plate of mac and cheese and apple slices in front of her right at 6:00, she reached out toward the side of my face as if she wanted to explore. I held still, ready to let her do that even as I winced at even the possibility of pain.

But she lowered her hand and went after the food.

After Lauren went to bed, the 10 o'clock news told me the dead man's name was Ralph Galloway. Their reporter Jeff Jenkins was live at the now-familiar scene. The crime scene tape was still up, and a couple cop cars were still there, and as Jenkins kept talking and the camera zoomed in toward Galloway's house, I couldn't help but wonder if inside, an officer might be gathering a stray hair or a drop of blood that might place me at the scene.

Jenkins said Galloway was discovered dead at the scene. As sorry as I felt for him, I was also, selfishly, relieved. If he'd still been alive and I hadn't done anything to help him, I'd never have forgiven myself.

Not a totally selfish reaction, now that I thought of it. Somewhere in the back of my mind, whenever I made an decision these days, I had to consider — how does this affect Lauren?

Never mind the almost daily risk of being caught while burglarizing someone's house, or that I was nearly caught at a murder scene! What, after all, happens to Lauren if I'm in the slammer?

I thrust that thought out of the way and returned my attention to the TV. A good thing, too, because that reporter, Jenkins, had turned his attention to a description of a vehicle seen leaving the crime scene just before the police arrived: "A white pickup truck, make and model unknown," he was saying, "was spotted by neighbors leaving the driveway of the deceased man's house, driven by a white male in his fifties. Anyone with information is asked to call the anonymous police tip line."

I stood up and stared at the TV. "Dammit!" I said, then covered my mouth and listened to see if I'd awakened Lauren.

I didn't hear anything; so far so good.

Jenkins' report was over — the newscast moved on to more gloom and doom. I turned off the TV and sat in the dark, arms folded, eyes closed, head back in my comfortable chair.

The police had no idea my "competitor" existed! If anything *I* was now the prime suspect in Ralph Galloway's death, although it seemed they didn't have much of a description of me or my pickup.

Still, could I even risk going out in my pickup anymore? How could I dare keep on with my burglary career? It was bad enough I'd discovered I had competition — now the eyes of the police would turn super-sensitive, block watches might form, and this entire part of town would be closed to my money-making efforts.

I didn't want to start over in another neighborhood — I'd invested too much time in this one. *But it's probably for the best*, I thought. *I'd be foolish not to seek out new territories, even if this hadn't happened. First my competitor essentially rips me off, getting that TV before me, then the shotgun granny about takes my head off, and now this.*

Is it even safe to drive my pickup through this part of town? Should I ditch it and buy a new one?

Right. What money are you gonna use to do that?

I opened my eyes and sat up, wringing my hands. I stopped. I looked down. My hands were shaking.

I know what I've got to do, I thought. *And if the thought of continuing my "career" in this neighborhood is a crazy one, this is even worse. I've got to start a new career, in a way.*

Because I had to wonder — if I *did* continue my life of crime, how many other times might I encounter this kid, and what would happen then? After all, I knew he wouldn't hesitate to kill.

I've got to do the police's work for them, I thought. *I've got to find this kid, the one who really killed poor Mr. Galloway. It's my only chance to get myself out of this situation.*

So I had to think. What did I know about this kid? If I could come up with something that I knew and the cops didn't, I'd have an advantage over them. I could find him and —

Then what? Kill him myself? No. I looked at my hands again. I was grateful that they'd stopped shaking. And also certain that I could never bring myself to wrap those hands around someone's neck and squeeze — unless someone was threatening Lauren. I'm many things, not all of them admirable, but I'm no killer.

Maybe I'm just getting ahead of myself, I thought. *Find the kid first. Then figure out what you're going to do with him.*

That settled that. But I couldn't do anything just yet. I pulled myself up out of my chair and went to bed and fell into a restless sleep, and dreamt of sunlight glinting off knives and guns being fired right into my face, and all the time Lauren sat quietly and played with her Barbies, not paying the least bit of attention to the danger I was in . . . .

. . . AND I AWOKE WITH A START.

The bowling shirts!

The kid, when he knocked me over the head and took off, had on the same kind of "Lucky Strikes" bowling shirt that I'd seen on the couch in the home where he'd taken that TV ahead of me. And poor dead Mr. Galloway's murder weapon was apparently a bowling trophy.

I threw back the covers, booted up my iMac, and opened up Google. A few keystrokes later, and I found that the "Lucky Strikes" bowling league was mostly retired fellows — not exactly the same demographic as my suspect.

But it was July — even if he was still in school, he'd be off for summer break. What if he was the son or grandson of someone in that league? I saw that they played at the That's How We Roll bowling alley, just about five miles away from my home. They gathered together mostly in the early afternoon at least a couple of days a week — including this very day.

Time to press the hunt.

AFTER I WALKED LAUREN TO DAYCARE, I STARTED formulating a plan to find this kid. I was hesitant to head right to That's How We Roll. I had no way of knowing how good a look he'd gotten of me as we grappled. And it's not as if I'm a master of disguise — I wasn't about to create a full-face mask, "Mission: Impossible" style and affect a French accent while gripping a cigarette holder and taking a big puff. Not that I smoke, or that Louisville's no-smoking laws would let me if I wanted to.

By the time the early afternoon rolled around, about the most I decided I could do was to put on a Ryder's Cup ball cap, pull it down as far as I could, and hope for the best.

But how the hell do I get there? I thought. I was afraid to head out in my pickup, worrying that it might as well have a big sign on it: MURDER SUSPECT ON BOARD. I didn't want to take a cab — it would be a stupid expense for short a trip and it would also provide a record that I'd visited the place — evidence I didn't want.

I even considered the bus, and went back to the computer to check out the schedules — turns out the bus comes by only a block from my home, but doesn't go any closer than five blocks to That's How We Roll.

Might as well walk, I thought, and in the end I did just that. It amounted to about an hour and a half's walk, and while I don't consider myself to be in bad shape (hauling around big-screen TVs on my own, remember), I'm not much of a walker. After about the first forty-five minutes, my calves were starting to hurt, and I had a stitch in my side that wouldn't go away. The Ohio River Valley humidity was taking its toll, too, with sweat streaming down my face and my entire body screaming for water — or better yet, a nice cold beer. *This is ridiculous*, I thought. *Some master burglar slash private eye you are.*

And dammit, not much of a planner, either. I've got to allow enough time to walk back to fetch Lauren from daycare.

By the time I trudged the distance to That's How We Roll, my strength was sapped, I was blinking against the sweat dripping down my face, and my feet were dragging. *I know for damn sure I'm not about to force some kind of confrontation with this kid*, I thought. *He'd whip my ass in about two seconds.*

Being a weekday afternoon, That's How We Roll's

parking lot wasn't crowded, which was probably why these retired guys played then. I tried to find a balance between pulling my cap down enough not to be recognized and not so much that I looked like I was trying not to be recognized.

All my senses were alert as I entered the bowling alley (eternally grateful for the blast of cool air that greeted me). I drew to a halt next to the bowling shoe rental counter, which stood to the right of the doorway, but my attention was focused on the other side of the room, on the bowling lanes. I was expecting to see that kid with a bunch of older guys, perhaps laughing nervously as he sat among them, a fish out of water, waiting for his turn at the lane.

And, sure enough, I quickly spotted the group of Lucky Strikes bowlers — they all appeared to be in their sixties, as I'd anticipated. And, as I expected, they were sitting, laughing, checking out each other's form (or lack of it) as they each took their turn.

But no kid.

Dammit, I thought. *Maybe he* is *a son or grandson of one of these guys, but he's at work or in summer school, and seldom comes here, and this is a dead end.*

"Sir? Can I help you? Do you need some shoes?"

The voice came directly from my right. The shoe rental counter. I actually started a little bit — I hadn't expected to speak to anyone, and didn't have a plausible cover story at hand. I turned and said, "No thank you, I'm just — "

It was the kid! Same blonde shoulder-length hair, same sideburns, same earring in the left ear.

" — just looking for a friend," I said, lowering my head, hoping he wouldn't notice the bruises he'd made on my face.

"Do I know him? What's his name?"

"That's all right," I said, turning away from the kid and

tenting my hand over my eyes as if staring into the sun, or a spotlight. "I can see he's not here." And I started to walk away without turning back toward him.

"Let us know if there's anything we can do for you, sir," the kid said as I reached the door. "I'll be on break soon, but anyone else can help you." I raised my hand in a casual wave as I went back out into the heat and humidity.

———————

I HAD ANOTHER HOUR AND A HALF WALK BACK HOME TO LOOK forward to. I made a quick stop in a convenience store to grab a bottled water. I glanced at the lottery tickets as I was checking out, but thought, *No, with my recent luck I'd end up owing the lottery a hundred million dollars.*

So I walked, and drank, and thought. *So the son-of-a-bitch works at That's How We Roll. Thank goodness he didn't seem to recognize me!*

And since he works there, he knows when the Lucky Strike players are there, and not at home — and, especially, which ones might be widowed or divorced, meaning no one else is at home.

And he was just going on break while they were there — that's when he pulls off his jobs.

So what do I do now? The damn kid about spooked me just asking me a question — I'm still not about to go back and try to threaten him or something.

And even if I did — he's shown he'll kill. I can't afford to make myself — and therefore make Lauren — a target.

It was too much to think about, and for a moment I just concentrated on walking, on taking the occasional sip of water, and trying not to think of what was next. Because all the alternatives seemed like bad ones.

I heard the screeching tires just as I stepped off the

pavement to cross a side street. My heart jumped, and I turned my head to look toward the source of that sound even as I tried to backstep toward the curb again.

Something struck me in the shoulder and whipped me around. I spun once and hit the pavement. I managed to look up just in time to see an SUV speeding away — the screeching tires hadn't been from the SUV trying to stop — it had been *accelerating*.

And I'd have sworn, looking at the back of the driver's head, that I saw a familiar shock of long blonde hair and the glint of an earring.

"Hey, young fella — are you OK?"

An older man was approaching me — although he was using a cane, he was surprisingly spry, perhaps more than I felt. "I'm all right," I said, though I didn't know if I was or not. I raised myself from the pavement and stood there a moment grasping my shoulder, trying to will the pain to go away.

I squinted into the distance and tried to make out the SUV that had struck me, but it was lost in traffic. The old man said, "I think he just clipped ya with his mirror — you were pretty lucky!"

"Yeah. Thanks." *I don't feel very damn lucky*, I thought as I hobbled away. I looked very carefully in each direction before crossing the street; I was afraid the kid would come back around for a second shot.

Was that actually him, I wondered, *or I am just getting paranoid?*

During the time I made the hour and a half walk back home, I decided I didn't care. The entire time, most of my thoughts were for Lauren. If I was a target, so was she, and that was unthinkable. I had a decision to make.

In the end, I did what was best for my girl; and that meant Doing The Right Thing.

Dammit.

I DECIDED I COULDN'T WAIT UNTIL MORNING — I DIDN'T HAVE any idea how serious the kid might be about killing me. So once I got home, I called Karen and asked if she could watch Lauren, maybe for a couple of days.

"Sure," she said. "But what's this about?"

"Can't tell you just yet," I said. "See you in a few minutes."

So I picked up Lauren from daycare, and despite what seemed to be the unconscionable risk of driving across town in my so-conspicuous crime-mobile, I got her to Karen's apartment without being pulled over.

"I wish you'd tell me what's going on, Phil," Karen said as we stood in her living room. Lauren was already sitting on the floor picking through a stack of books. Karen, I knew, loved story time with Lauren as much she did. "You're worrying me."

"No reason to be worried," I told her, the first time, I think, I've ever lied right to her face. "I'll be able to tell you more soon." I went to Lauren and leaned over gave her a hug, which she didn't return. A quick peck on the cheek for Karen, as I managed not to look her in the eyes, and I left.

Got in the truck.

Headed right to the corner of Seventh and Jefferson, downtown.

Louisville Metro Police Headquarters.

I parked at a meter, but didn't put in any money. I figured either that small offense would eventually be forgiven or wouldn't much matter when I was sitting in a cold prison cell.

———

SO, ULTIMATELY, THE CONCLUSION OF MY LITTLE ADVENTURE in crime was pretty simple. Guy becomes burglar, guy is attacked by murderer, guy turns in murderer, guy starts new life as upstanding citizen.

My initial talk with detectives didn't go as quickly as I thought it would — seems I had some explaining to do, after I was Mirandized and told them repeatedly I was waiving my right to a lawyer. "Lemme get this straight," my questioner, Det. Edward Galvan, said as we sat in a stark, brightly lit interrogation room. He was trying to pull the good-cop routine, but the more I looked into his eyes, the more I could see his heart wasn't in it. "You're here to turn yourself in — to confess to these burglaries?"

"Well, yeah, sort of. But mostly I'm here to tell you about this other guy — the one who committed the Galloway murder. And I can't do that without telling you why I was in Galloway's house right after he was killed."

"So you're trying to cut a deal."

"What I'm trying to do is save my life, and maybe my daughter's." And I explained about Lauren and her autism and how my life of crime had begun. Galvan's eyes held a little more sympathy now, though I never doubted it was for Lauren, not me.

After hearing my story, they went right out and picked up "the kid," finding him at That's How We Roll — his name was Greg Angelino, and it turned out he wasn't that much of a kid, just a very young-looking 24 years old.

He'd played out pretty much the same pattern I had —

not being able to find a decent job, having too many bills, turning to burglary as a last resort. But he took a nasty turn I never did, and like to believe never would. He didn't start out robbing from people he knew. That came later, as he became more desperate for money. The person he stole the big screen TV from before I could snatch it was a friend of his uncle's — a fellow bowler whose "Lucky Strike" shirt I'd seen on the couch.

Angelino waited until the guy showed up at That's How We Roll, took his lunch break, then ripped him off.

The murder victim, Ralph Galloway, was another friend of his uncle's, another bowler. Except Galloway had a tendency toward an upset stomach sometimes, and the day — the hour — that Angelino picked to burglarize his home was one of those times. He returned home, surprised Angelino, they scuffled, and Angelino picked up that bowling trophy with his gloved hand and bashed in Galloway's head with it.

Based on my information, the cops got a search warrant for Angelino's home and found a shirt with Galloway's blood spatter on it. He should'a made that trip to the dumpster. That, and my testimony, locked things up pretty well, and Angelino took a plea, both on the murder and the several burglaries he'd done. Without my testimony, it might've taken some time for the police to figure out what was going on. Angelino said Galloway was only the second burglary he'd attempted based on someone being at the bowling alley, and he said he was going to give up that M.O. when he got the nerve to commit another one.

But what would happen to me, now?

All I cared about was that Lauren was safe. It was never about me. Everything I did, both the bad — the burglaries

— and the good — turning in Angelino even though it meant surrendering my own freedom — I did for her.

———

"Do you have any idea how pissed I was?" Karen asked. We were teaming up to wash the dishes after a home-cooked meal I'd prepared for us to celebrate my freedom. She washed, I dried. "I had no idea my brother was a professional criminal." She turned and peered into the living room, where Lauren was curled up with a Harry Potter book I'd read to her at least twice and which I think she was reading for a third time on her own. Quietly, she said, "And as much as I love Lauren, I wasn't sure I wanted to become a full-time surrogate mom so quickly."

"I'm sorry I put that on you."

"Well — I got over being pissed when I realized you were having it a lot tougher than I was — serves you right, by the way!"

"I just didn't want the state taking her — she needed the same toys, same kitchen, same walk to daycare every day."

Karen handed me a dripping plate. "None of that matters now. You're back home, and that's all that counts."

As I toweled the plate dry, I said, "As long as I remain a good boy."

My lawyer and I had gotten me a good deal, which because of my service to the community in helping take a killer off the streets, amounted to no time in jail, restitution for all my victims, and probation for five years, then everything dropped.

I was determined to remain a good boy.

Which was easier than I'd feared. In fact, my newfound celebrity, or perhaps notoriety, had worked in my favor. I'd given the reporter who'd been on the scene of the Galloway murder, Jeff Jenkins, an exclusive interview, and the next day the phone started to ring. I could tell most of the book and movie deals were scams, but I accepted a position with a security agency that was interested in my "expertise" in crime, and I was hoping to start up my own firm once I was off probation.

Karen and I finished the dishes, each grabbed ourselves a beer, and sat in the living room watching Lauren, who was still engrossed in her book. In fact, I could've sworn she was smiling, just a little bit.

I told Karen, "You know, there's only one thing I miss about my old job as criminal — the thrill of casing those homes, of being inside them and taking the risk of someone hearing me or seeing me, of getting away with something."

"Remember the part about being a good boy?"

"I know. Anytime I get once of those urges, I think of Lauren. They go away pretty quickly."

I took a long draw of beer and said, "I'm making enough money now that I can afford a few things, which is good because I have to pay back everyone I burglarized from. I can remember all the homes I broke into and what I took from them. I'm in the process of buying replacements for everything I stole — in some cases, like TVs, I'm even trading up, with the latest equipment."

"Why, Phillip, that's great — that's admirable."

"But I'm still resisting that one urge," I said. "Can you imagine how surprised my former victims would be when they got home to realize a burglar had broken in to *return* their stuff?"

IN PLAIN SIGHT

This introduction could be longer than the story if I'm not careful. Suffice it to say that Detective Galvan, whom you've met before in this collection, and will meet again later, has to have a sharp eye for detail to solve his latest case.

———

Detective Edward Galvan was in such a hurry he nearly ran into a large ceramic planter as he rushed into the Hall of Justice, headed toward the crime scene. He flashed his shield so the sheriff's deputies working the metal detector would let him pass, but he had to pause as a group of jurors returning from an auxiliary courthouse went around the detector ahead of him.

The crime scene was a men's rest room on the second floor. Galvan nodded to a couple uniformed officers he knew as he entered. He recognized the body on the floor -- prosecutor Daniel Lawson. "Damn," he said. "Daniel was a good guy. A good prosecutor."

Crime scene investigator Katie Melendez, who was kneeling next to Daniel, said, "We found the murder weapon." She indicated a handgun in a clear plastic evidence bag on the floor.

"Any witnesses?" Galvan asked.

"Apparently Daniel and the shooter were all alone."

Galvan kneeled down and took a good look at the murder weapon. "Any prints?"

"None."

"The grip is dirty."

"Saw that," Katie said. "Don't know if it means anything."

Galvan said, "Even as I was coming here, the computer folks said they were cross-referencing Daniel's recent cases to see who might've held a grudge."

Katie stood. "That's likely to be a long list."

Galvan's cell phone buzzed. "Galvan."

"Detective, this is Julie Thomas — computer lab. We made an odd connection while we were looking into Prosecutor Lawson's recent cases."

"Odd? In what way?"

"There's a fellow named Zachary Miller whose brother, Chester, he put away a few months ago. Drug-related murder. Zachary's right there in the Hall of Justice -- in the jury pool!"

Galvan grabbed a uniformed officer. "Get to the jury room — don't let them clear it!"

A FEW MINUTES LATER, GALVAN ENTERED THE JURY ROOM. THE uniforms had detained Zachary Miller. Two of them flanked the man, who was sitting in a hard plastic chair. Miller asked, "So why are we here?"

"It seems odd that you'd happen to be on jury duty the day a prosecutor you have a grudge against is killed."

"Coincidences happen."

Galvan said, "You've been a suspect in everything from drug cases to weapons charges. I'd think the computer would've kicked your name out."

"Suspected — never charged, Detective. No reason I shouldn't be here doing my civic duty."

Galvan said, "I'm told you're a 'computer whiz.' Is that how someone gets himself *onto* jury duty instead of avoiding it? And makes sure he's scheduled into the auxiliary courthouse away from the Hall of Justice, but knowing he'll have to return here later?"

"How would I get a gun into the Hall of Justice?"

"I've figured out *exactly* how you did it," Galvan said. "I dodged a planter as I was coming here just now. That's where you stashed the gun ahead of time. I saw the dirt still embedded in part of its grip. You grabbed it as your jury came back from the auxiliary courthouse. I was told you never wanted to get your hands dirty when it came to your brother's business. But in this case you did."

"If you're so smart," Miller said, "how'd I get the gun here into the Hall of Justice?"

"Jurors coming from the auxiliary courthouse get to bypass the metal detector. After you shot Lawson, you 'hid' in plain sight in the jury room." Galvan motioned for Miller to stand. He got out his handcuffs and slapped them onto Miller's hands. "I don't think we'll have any trouble finding you from now on, though."

MARLOWE, HIT MAN

THIS IS ONE OF THOSE STORIES THAT BEGAN WITH A TITLE that just appeared to me out of thin air -- one of those gifts that reality provides for you if you're lucky. This title was too delicious not to write a story to go with it.

MY NAME'S MARLOWE. AT LEAST THAT'S WHAT I CALL MYSELF. And no, it's not after the famous Raymond Chandler character. Chandler's Marlowe was a great detective, one of the "good guys." Most people wouldn't consider a hit man one of the good guys. No, my alias, professional name, nom de guerre, if you will, is after the great poet and playwright Christopher Marlowe. And you may recall that Chandler's Marlowe also enjoyed poetry, so maybe there's a bit of symmetry there.

Why him? Why not the big name, the real superstar, ole Willy Shakespeare? I've never been sure. All I know is that Marlowe's words do for my soul -- if I still have one -- what this glass of bourbon is doing right now for my shaking hands. I need both every time after a hit. I guess this time more than most.

I'm okay while I'm actually doing the work. At the moment I sight down the scope, ready to squeeze the trigger, my hands are steady, my breathing stilled, my heartbeat muted. Then, finally, squeeze! And recoil! And, often as not, the reassuring sound of a round punching through an office window or a car windshield -- man, it's like nothing else.

And behind that window or windshield, that lovely red blossom, blooming only for an instant before destroying itself with a splash, but what an instant! It has all the finality of one of Christopher Marlowe's finely-wrought phrases, such as "the malice of the angry skies" or "faithful love will never turn to hate."

Did you know there's a beautiful rose called the Christopher Marlowe? Its petals make an orange-red splash against your consciousness when you first glimpse it. I can't grow a single flower in my own backyard, but I can create a splash of beauty rivaling anything in nature.

But tonight was tougher than most. This shoot was personal. Here's how it began:

My boss, Daniel Drake, is what you might call a crime lord. But he doesn't take cuts from whores or drug dealers, he doesn't send thugs to manhandle store owners to get them to sign up for "protection." His underlings aren't packing heat and they aren't wearing suits that don't quite fit right or muttering threats to you while puffing on a stogie. No, he's more modern -- internet fraud, identity theft, intellectual property infringement. He has staff, not minions, a bunch of millennials who wear t-shirts with obscure internet memes or logos of steaming TV shows I've never heard of. Me, I've still got my Led Zeppelin and Beatles shirts.

But don't think he won't get violent when he feels he needs to. That's where I come in.

Everyone's greedy sometime or another. Sometimes that greed means you take the biggest of the complimentary rolls from the basket at the steakhouse. It's why mothers tell one kid he can slice a too-large piece of pie in half, but his brother gets to pick which piece he wants.

Sometimes greed makes unscrupulous people steal from Mr. Drake. A few keystrokes here, a bit of virtual currency rerouted there, and suddenly Mr. Drake is a few hundred thousand or even a million short.

Mr. Drake doesn't like that. If it's small potatoes, Mr. Drake might make sure someone has a good talking-to, might give him the chance to say it was all a big mistake and he'll never do it again.

And sometimes they do it again. That's when all of a sudden they don't show up for work in their nice, soft, silvery office and everyone wonders what happened to Derek or Justin or Jennifer.

That's when I was doing my job.

Either way, Mr. Drake hides his involvement in any death or disappearance associated with someone who pisses him off. He always manages to fly under the radar, whether it's cops or other crooks hoping to detect what he's up to. He's weathered his share of dangers, whether indictments or assassination attempts.

Last week, though, he gave me my latest assignment. And I balked.

At first, it seemed just like the dozen other assignments we've talked about over the years. My cover story as a "security consultant" lets me meet with Mr. Drake in his cavernous office which takes up a considerable portion of the 54th floor of his skyscraper headquarters. High windows overlooking a cityscape beneath oncoming storm clouds. Plush, tasteful carpeting that muted even the heaviest footfall. Computer-generated white noise that Mr. Drake said keeps him calm.

His desk was on one side of the room, a laptop computer the only thing sitting upon it. No landline, no stacks of papers, no pictures of loved ones. We sat in the center of the room; Mr. Drake doesn't like barriers between himself and people he's speaking with.

He poured me a generous glass of the best bourbon, handed me a cigar made with 18-year-old tobacco and enhanced with Cognac. Purely for later enjoyment, since Mr. Drake doesn't allow smoking in his facilities. He ran his fingers through his movie-star-quality black hair and gave me a piercing stare. "So, Marlowe, this mission's a different one for you."

I let a sip of bourbon flow down my throat, its heat a comfort. "I can handle different."

Mr. Drake's mouth spread in a wide smile that his eyes didn't reflect. "This isn't someone who's tried to rip me off, or one of my 'competitors.' Someone different. An actor."

My raised eyebrows indicated my increased attention. "Anyone I would know?"

"Not personally. But you know his work. A fella named Arthur Weller."

I tried not to show overt emotion, but couldn't help taking in a deep breath. Weller had appeared years earlier in a one-man show based on Christopher Marlowe's works, performing key scenes from his plays and reciting segments of his poetry. I'd already revered Marlowe, but Weller's performance helped seal the deal on my obsession with him.

I let that deep breath out slowly. "What's your beef with Weller?"

Mr. Drake gaze fell toward the floor. He rubbed a hand across his face. I was doubly shocked now; I'd never seen him reveal any emotion other than total confidence before. Finally he said, "Weller's having . . . let's say, 'an affair' with Angela."

I sat up straighter in my chair. Everything made sense now. If Mr. Drake had one weakness, it was Angela Cuvier. Before her, he'd involved himself with a series of women I thought of as stereotypes -- bubbly blondes, hot redheads, swimsuit models.

Angela was different. A dark-skinned beauty from France, she possessed two doctorates -- one in geology, the other in astrophysics, of all things. She described her interests as beginning deep underground and heading toward the stars. I knew all that only because Mr. Drake had told me. He wouldn't let me meet her, saying he didn't want her "around the likes of you, with all respect."

Yeah, I guess I have to respect that. If I want to keep getting paid.

"So you think that if I get rid of Weller -- "

Mr. Drake nodded. "She'll come back to me. I know she will."

I couldn't share my own doubts regarding that outcome. Again, getting paid and all that. But to kill Arthur Weller!

I guess I didn't hide my concern as well as I thought. "You don't have a problem with that, do you? Killing Weller, I mean."

I shook my head slowly. "Nope. A job's a job."

Mr. Drake wagged a finger at me. "Good. I know your usual routine. Keep to it." My usual routine meant going about my business and never speaking to him about it again.

I even had the leeway to change the assignment if circumstances changed, to let someone off with a hard warning on the one hand, or to add a second or even third target on the other. We both gulped the remnants of our bourbon, stood, and shook hands. I left, making the long silent walk across the office, hoping that nothing in my gait or the way I swung my arms or reached for the doorknob revealed my severe doubts about the whole assignment.

NORMALLY I'D WOULDN'T LET MYSELF BE DISTRACTED FROM MY latest job. I'd go right home and find out all I could about him if he had a significant online presence. And who doesn't these days? At first, I did just that, and for Arthur Weller, it was particularly easy. The man was a actor who'd starred in a number roles on stage, and in television and movies. While never a huge star, he worked consistently. In the past six months alone, he'd been the lead in a small independent movie and a guest star on *Law & Order: SVU*. His next gig, in a couple weeks, looked to be a *Star Trek: Discovery* episode, which would take him to Toronto for filming.

My job was to make sure he never made it there.

That's when the distractions creeped in.

My fingers paused over my computer keyboard as the memories of Arthur Weller's performance of my namesake's words washed over me. Whether it was that other Marlowe's ode to Helen of Troy, and her "face that launch'd a thousand ships," or Dr. Faustus lamenting "In being deprived of everlasting bliss," Weller's enthusiasm and respect for Marlowe's words shone through in every syllable uttered by his mellifluous voice and the most subtle emotion conveyed through the slightest parting of his mouth or a single raised eyebrow.

I didn't want to still that voice, those features. But this was my job. I decided that, in respect for him, my performance would have to be the equal of his, and that I must dispatch him humanely, in an instant, and without pain.

OVER THE NEXT FEW WEEKS I SHADOWED WELLER, LEARNING his routine. He often stayed up until the wee hours and didn't stir until late morning, a habit perhaps reinforced by evening stage performances. He usually shopped for groceries at the same small neighborhood store, went out for drinks with the same two or three friends, at least one of whom I recognized from a recurring role on a basic cable sitcom.

On Tuesdays and Fridays he would meet with Angela, always at the same restaurant, an Italian joint about a mile and a half from Weller's apartment. He always walked, perhaps his way to keep in shape. She always arrived in a cab or an Uber.

Weller habitual order is the Seafood Ravioli, which he wolfs it down as if he was ravenous. Angela alternates between the Pasta Fresca and the Cajun Pasta, never finishes either dish, and always requests a take-home box. Then they retreat to Weller's apartment. Angela stays the night about half the time.

I had to wonder what made Angela so enamored of two such different men as Arthur Weller and Mr. Drake. That curiosity made me break one of my most sacred rules -- I placed myself in a position where they might notice me.

I visited that restaurant one Tuesday night, requesting that the server place me at a certain booth because I liked the view of the street scene outside. Actually, it was because it was next to Weller and Angela's usual booth.

It was only because Angela had never met me that I took this risk; as it was, I felt like the goofy neighbor in a movie comedy who was spying on his best friend. I also discovered that there really isn't a way to hide your face behind your menu without looking like you're trying to hide your face behind your menu. So I remained as still as I could while Angela and Weller took their seats right behind me. She chuckled at some comment from Weller I couldn't make out as I ordered the Chicken Parmigiana.

Weller and Angela placed their orders moments later -- the usual Seafood Ravioli for him, and apparently it was Pasta Fresca night for Angela. Her backrest was on the other side of my own as I strained to make out their voices against the backdrop of other customers' background conversation, clinking wine glasses, and the flop-flop sound of the swinging doors at the entrance to the kitchen. But by the time my own food arrived, my goal of gaining any insight as to why Angela was interested in both Weller and Mr. Drake remained unfulfilled. I'd nearly resigned myself to simply enjoying a good meal when Angela's voice caught my attention.

No single word signaled the change; rather, it was that Angela spoke more quietly and with a more somber tone. "I've told you about my other boyfriend," she told Weller.

I could hear the smile in Weller's voice: "I'm just glad I count as a boyfriend at all."

"You're much more liberal than Daniel. He wouldn't like it if he knew about you. I'll have to do something about that."

A pause before Weller spoke again, and this time I didn't hear the smile. "You're not breaking up with me, are you?"

Through my backrest, I felt Angela lean toward Weller. "Of course not, dear. It's Daniel who's getting that news. I don't know what I was thinking even becoming involved with him. Maybe I've spent too much of my life in academics. Becoming immersed in the business world through him was fascinating for awhile. I've even heard the faintest hints of him being involved in illegal activities."

The hand that held my fork paused halfway to my mouth.

Angela continued: "I don't believe a bit of it, of course. But it did add a bit of spice to the relationship. He's not used to being contradicted, though. Maybe I'll just try to scale back my relationship with him at first."

You'd never believe all the emotions Angela's words evoked in me. I knew that if she made even the slightest attempt to "scale back" her relationship with Mr. Drake, that my assignment immediately after Arthur Weller's demise would be to eliminate Angela. And I'd never refused an assignment. If I were going to, I'd have done it with Weller.

But I knew my current assignment had to change drastically, and that I I couldn't waste any time. The hardest part, I knew, would be telling myself I was remaining true to Mr. Drake's insistence that I retain some leeway in my assignment. The hard warning on the one hand or the second or third target on the other.

I didn't dare delay that decision. But once made, I could only hope I wouldn't regret it.

I'M OKAY WHILE I'M ACTUALLY DOING THE WORK. USUALLY. This time, across the street from my target, I sighted down the scope, ready to squeeze the trigger. But my hands were far from steady. The shaking that normally only affected my glass of bourbon after the fact had arrived prematurely. I closed my eyes, fought to still those hands. Like I said earlier, this was tougher than most. This was personal.

Christopher Marlowe's words came to me, from "The Passionate Shepherd to his Love":

The Shepherds' Swains shall dance and sing

For thy delight each May-morning:

If these delights thy mind may move,

Then live with me, and be my love.

I had to wonder, as my hands finally stilled and I sighted down the scope again, whether Arthur Weller had ever thought of these words as he made love to Angela Cuvier, or whether he'd ever recited them to her over glasses of wine.

I squeezed the trigger, felt the recoil, and there it was -- that lovely red blossom, that bloom that existed only for an instant before resolving into a splash.

Even across the street, I could hear the alarms going off in Mr. Drake's building. I lingered in the shadows only long enough to see his security people bursting into his office. I faded away before they could catch a glimpse of me.

No time for that glass of bourbon this time, I had to get the hell out of town. Years ago I'd spent some of Mr. Drake's generous fees in setting up an alternate identity for myself, building a home in a remote area of Colorado, and installing plenty of alarm systems both in the home and in all the possible approaches to it, whether down the only gravel-covered road or across an open field or through a forest. My assumption, however, had been that I'd be protecting myself against one of Mr. Drake's associates, not the great man himself, or at least his minions.

As I retreated westward in the car bearing my alternate identity on its registration, I hoped for all the best for Arthur Weller and Angela Cuvier, who were left with two mysteries to ponder -- who killed Mr. Drake, and who left the large bouquet of Christopher Marlowe flowers at Weller's doorstep?

I smiled at the memory of the instant I placed them there, as I couldn't help but run my hands gently across several of the flowers' petals, the tips of my fingers seemingly communicating that orange-red splash against my consciousness, even with my eyes closed.

BEYOND JUSTICE

TWO MEN GRIEVING THE LOSS OF FAMILY MEMBERS REACH OUT to one another, one more enthusiastically than the other. But will either find comfort in this new relationship?

———

THE DARK WOOD OF THE WALLS IN THE VISITATION ROOM IS muted. Matt feels as if it's designed to absorb all the color and all the emotions from its surroundings.

Why, he wonders, *do such rooms never have windows? Wouldn't it be a comfort to see sunlight streaming in, to feel its warmth? Wouldn't it connect us to that broader world that still awaits us after this ritual of remembrance ends?*

Then, his next thought: *Perhaps that's the point. We release our grief into this room, then we release ourselves back into the world, squinting into the sunlight.*

But Matt realizes that isn't working. The only emotions anyone has expressed about the sudden death of his wife Diane and daughter Megan are quiet condolences. He expects more from these friends, even though it's been years since he's seen some of them.

There's Gene, for instance -- he and Matt had shared joints all through college, thirty years ago now, and he'd slept with his sister a couple of times back then. When those close encounters were revealed, Matt had been afraid he'd be pissed, but Gene just laughed, saying he was glad two people he loved were having a good time.

On this day, however, Gene provides only a loose, shoulders-only hug and some obvious platitudes about how great a woman Diane was and how much potential Megan had.

Then there were Bob and Annie from work, the two of them constant jokesters who help one another as well as Matt make it through the long days at their big box store, dealing on the one hand with managers who regard them all with suspicion, fearful they may spend half a minute away from their tasks, and on the other hand with customers demanding concierge-style service from minimum-wage workers.

As Bob and Annie approach Matt, they're poking each other in the ribs as they try, mostly unsuccessfully, to suppress laughter. "Sorry," Annie says through a final giggle. "We really are sorry." Each of them manages to maintain appropriately sad expressions as they deliver some worthy platitudes of their own. The instant they walk away, though, the poking and giggling start up again.

Matt wonders if these reactions are due to the shock, the suddenness of Diane and Megan's deaths. Dark, narrow mountain road on the way back from a trip to her parents, two states away. Drunk driver, Patricia Van Buren, coming the opposite direction on a curve near her own home. The crash.

Matt hesitates to take another glance at his two loved ones in their caskets, to stand over them and stare down one more time at their still features.

I don't want to imagine Diane's face not engaged in constant movement, he thinks. *I'm so accustomed to her eyebrows arching upward when we disagree, her mouth sketching a sideways smile after one of my lame jokes, her hands gesturing every which-way as she tries to make a point.*

And Megan -- how could I think of seeing her when she wasn't tilting her head to one side and rolling her eyes as she listens to one of my parental rants, or making those furtive glances at me and getting up from the living room couch when her latest boyfriend calls? But also coming to me on the couch and curling up next to me without a word needed.

I know why I'm so numb, he thinks. *I need someone to blame. The obvious target would be Patricia Van Buren. But she's dead, too, and she's beyond any idea of justice.*

It's a void Matt is just becoming aware he's trying to fill.

A stranger enters the visitation room, looks around, and his eyes widen with recognition as he spots Matt. Walks toward him with purpose. But as the man stares into Matt's eyes, he struggles to find words. Is this some co-worker of Diane's, or the parent of one of Megan's friends?

The man's suit is nicely tailored, while Matt's is a bit threadbare. The other man walks toward him with a confidence that tells Matt this is someone much more accustomed to such dress. For his part, Matt has spent much of his time pulling at his collar and re-centering his tie.

The man reaches Matt, extends his hand: "I had to come here. I had to tell you how sorry I was. I'm . . . Frederick Van Buren."

The drunk driver's husband. *Now* all the pent-up emotions surge within Matt, everything that's been building since that knock on the door at two in the morning that revealed a police officer and a chaplain. Since the failure of denial. Since having to cope with arrangements and countless other practicalities all alone, as an only child whose parents had passed years earlier and who isn't close to other family members.

He jerks his hand from Van Buren's grasp, and is about to release that surge of emotions in an angry confrontation - - why the hell would this man come here to add to his grief? How could he ever think he's someone whose presence could give him some comfort?

But he imagines Diane's hand on his shoulder, stopping him cold. Of course she would intuit his reaction and with a whisper into his ear would delay his outburst just for one moment, that single moment that would let his initial reaction subside.

Matt's voice is calmer than he imagined: "What do you want?"

Van Buren swallows. Licks his lips. "Only . . . to tell you how sorry I am. I never knew your wife, your daughter, of course. But I've seen the pictures of them on TV. Your wife looked to be so kind. I could see it in her eyes. I know she had to be a good mother. And your daughter -- I bet she was devoted to you."

As he speaks, Van Buren's gaze falls from Matt's face, and Matt perceives guilt in those eyes. He finds his anger beginning to fade, even as he wills himself to hold onto it as the only thing that anchors his emotions right now.

But he can't sustain that. *This man's not responsible for what his wife did,* he thinks. *And he has his own grieving to do, his own sense of that void he needs to fill.*

Matt takes a deep breath. Decides to take the high road.

"Well, Mr. Van Buren, I appreciate those thoughts. I imagine it took a bit of courage to come here."

Van Buren looks at Matt again. "Actually, I didn't have the courage to live with myself if I hadn't come here."

Matt can only nod and give Van Buren a wan smile. Van Buren tells Matt, "I'll be thinking of you in my prayers." He looks away from Matt, turns, and heads for the hallway.

TWO DAYS LATER. MATT TRUDGES INTO HIS EMPTY HOME JUST after 1:30 in the morning, replenishing stock hours after the store closed.

Anything to keep from facing his grief straight-on. He wonders when he'll be able to let himself cry.

He pours a glass of milk because it's easier than making a cup of coffee or tea. Takes those couple of steps to the kitchen table. Moves aside a laptop computer to make room for his milk. Sits.

The past few months, he'd already been missing Megan's presence after she'd gone away to college. But at least Diane had still been here, and even now his ears strained to hear the squeaking of bedsprings, the padding of bare feet from the bedroom. She always got up to give him a hug and a kiss on the cheek and ask about his day, even when when it meant less sleep for her when she arose for her early morning departure to her grocery store job.

After a couple of sips of milk, Matt's mind begins to engage again, but his thoughts head down paths he doesn't want to explore just yet.

Without thinking, he pulls the laptop close and starts it up.

Home page: Facebook. He scrolls past more

condolences, some from people who showed up for the visitation and funeral, others from people who didn't.

After a moment, Matt spots the red notification at the top of the screen. Friend request. He clicks on it.

Frederick Van Buren.

Goddam no, is his first thought and his right hand darts to the touchpad, but it's shaking with so much emotion that he can't center the cursor on the offending dot.

He lets go the mouse and grasps his right hand with his left. And again the anger begins to fade, and he realizes that from outside this empty house, someone has reached out to him in shared grief.

Another moment of hesitation, then he clicks ACCEPT. Goes to bed, as always lying on "his" side, despite Diane's absence. As he slips into sleep, he wonders whether he'll ever find it natural to lie in the middle of the bed.

———

THE NEXT MORNING, MATT'S CELL RINGS AS HE ROAMS through a grocery, trying to focus on what items he's low on at home. He shifts a package of toilet paper and a carton of eggs onto his left arm as he fumbles with his right hand to retrieve the phone, thinking he should've gotten a cart.

It's Frederick Van Buren.

Shit, Matt thinks. The Facebook friending was more than enough. He asks, "How'd you get this number?"

Frederick says "lawyer friends" found it for him, and he hopes he hasn't caught Matt at a bad moment.

Matt lets Frederick know he hasn't had a lot of good moments lately, and that he's busy in the grocery.

"It's not the grocery where . . . ."

"Where Diane worked? No." He doesn't want to elaborate

to Frederick that he doesn't want to have to listen to her co-workers telling him how sorry they are.

"Listen," Frederick says, "I'd like to get together with you."

Matt stops cold in the middle of an aisle. A woman pushing an overflowing grocery cart gives him a dirty look as she squeezes past him. "Why would you suggest that?" Matt says.

Frederick says, "The two of us could console one another."

"You worried a minute ago about whether I should go to my wife's grocery. But now I should spend time with the husband of the woman who killed my family?"

"I'm dealing with my own issues, you know. Mostly guilt, though I know I have no reason to be guilty. It tortures me."

Matt searches mentally for a way to blow off the idea, but then Frederick says, "The police have been speaking to me about Patricia. About how much I knew about her drinking."

Matt considers this while clutching his toilet paper and eggs tightly as a couple more shoppers squeeze past him. Finally he tells Frederick, "How about tomorrow at noon? A place called Charlie Winston's. You can look it up."

"I'll be there," Frederick says.

As Frederick hangs up, Matt wonders what he's gotten himself into.

MORE DARK WALLS, IS ONE OF MATT'S FIRST THOUGHTS AS HE sits across from Frederick at Charlie Winston's. His furtive glances around tell him that jeans are, although acceptable here, worn only by a minority. I'd bet a lot of these nicely dressed fellas in here make more in a month than I do in a year, he thinks, noting Frederick's own immaculate suit, a different one from the one he wore to Diane and Megan's funeral.

A waiter arrives to take their drink order and Frederick orders something called a Caipirninha. "It's kind of like a daiquiri," he tells Matt, who orders whatever's on draft.

As the waiter departs, Frederick buries his head in the menu as Matt looks on. Eventually Frederick, from behind the menu, asks whether Matt's ever been to his restaurant before.

Matt explains he's more of a McDonald's or Wendy's kinda guy. Maybe Steak 'n Shake, if he has coupons.

When the drinks arrive, the waiter asks for their food orders. Frederick orders the Garlic-Rosemary Cornish game hen.

Matt takes a final look at his own copy of the extensive menu and says, "Chicken fingers." He could swear the waiter looks disdainfully at his jeans and takes the menu from him as if it's contaminated.

With no menu to act as shield, Frederick's gaze darts around the room. He rubs his hands together, taps his fingers on the table, then forces his palms down flat. Matt is content to sit in silence and watch this drama play out.

Frederick swallows. Licks his lips. *This is a replay of the scene from the visitation room,* Matt thinks.

Finally Frederick asks Matt how he's holding together.

I still haven't cried, Matt thinks, but isn't about to say that to this man.

Frederick pushes on. "I mean, I know what it's like to lose your wife. But you lost your daughter, too."

A silence lengthens, and Matt feels no need to fill it. *I made a mistake coming here,* he thinks.

Frederick takes another sip of his Caipirninha. Places

the glass back onto the table with a measured movement. Says, "The police are still asking questions. About Patricia."

Matt works to keep his expression neutral. He's determined to wait Frederick out.

Frederick pulls at his collar. The police, it seems, want to know often Patricia drank, how drunk she'd habitually get. He tells Matt, "The . . . uh . . . deaths of your wife and daughter are officially a homicide."

Matt tells Frederick he knows that.

Frederick reaches for his Caipirninha, takes a sip, lowers it partway. The glass partially obscures Frederick's face. "I wish I didn't feel so guilty."

After only a moment's hesitation, Matt asks, "Do you have anything to -- "

Frederick interrupts. "Of course not." He explains Patricia had been laid off from her job at a non-profit that collects food for underprivileged children.

Matt asks Frederick what he does. Work in securities, is the answer. Frederick says he's financially secure, but that Patricia was a bit of a clothes horse, and liked getting her hair and nails done at "fancy places." She'd run up a lot of credit card debt. "And I never noticed. Pretty dumb for someone who works in the financial field, huh?"

Matt has no reason to disagree, and no reason to state that out loud. He asks, "What do you want from me?"

Frederick runs his hands along the sides of his glass. "Just . . . someone who understands what I'm going through."

Matt sits back as the waiter brings their food. Frederick sits with a fork poised over his Garlic-Rosemary Cornish game hen, looking at if as if he'd ordered something different.

Matt pushes chicken fingers around on his plate. Out of the corner of his eye, he sees the first signs of a stir at the restaurant's entrance. A bit of movement, people whispering. Two uniformed police officers, a man and a woman, are entering, along with another man in plainclothes who also gives off that unmistakable vibe of law enforcement.

Frederick's back is to the entrance. "I don't think we're going to be friends," Matt tells him. Their waiter is speaking with the officers, pointing toward the table where Matt and Frederick are sitting. A nod from a uniformed officer, a two-fingered wave from the plainclothes one, and the three head toward their table, every customer's gaze following them. They're barely two steps away before Frederick notices.

The plainclothes officer looks at Frederick. "Anton Frederick Van Buren?"

Frederick puts down his fork, places both hands flat on the table, and straightens his back. "Yes, I'm Frederick Van Buren."

"Detective Edward Galvan. You're under arrest in connection with the murders of Diane Sullivan and Megan Sullivan . . . "

Matt gasps. How could Frederick be the one who killed his family? He wasn't even in the car.

Galvan continues: " . . . and Patricia Van Buren."

Matt stands and stares at Frederick, who is still sitting calmly, as if this turn of events is one he's expected. Frederick lifts his napkin, gently pats his mouth, and stands.

Galvan says, "Don't give us any trouble, and we'll do the cuffs outside."

"That's fair," Frederick says. To Matt, he says, "I really did feel guilty. My reaching out to you was sincere."

Galvan nods toward the uniformed officers and they lead Frederick toward the front of the restaurant. He looks at Matt. "You're Mr. Sullivan?"

Now it's Matt's turn to nod. It's all he can muster. It's difficult for him to absorb what Galvan tells him next, that Patricia Van Buren had no history of alcoholism, had never been treated for it, friends and neighbors saw no sign of it, and her autopsy showed no sign of long-term alcohol abuse.

The marital troubles, Galvan explains, including the loss of her job and the credit card debt, provided motive. Bruising on Patricia's arms and stomach were long-standing injuries, not suffered during the crash. Galvan says he believes Frederick forced a combination of bourbon and vodka down his wife's throat. Somehow he convinced her to drive away, perhaps with threats of more violence.

"He wanted to her to die," Galvan says. "But he never considered she might take someone else with her."

That someone was my family, Matt thinks, and he rushes toward the front of the restaurant and pounds Frederick from behind with both his fists.

It's only as the uniformed officers and Galvan pull him off Frederick and he starts to sink to the floor that he realizes that void within him is finally filled and, heedless of all the eyes upon him, the tears begin to flow.

THE CONTRARY DETECTIVE

I WORKED FOR NEARLY FOUR DECADES IN THE LOCAL TV NEWS business, so I couldn't resist setting a mystery story in that world. I took a couple liberties here in how "the biz" actually works, but I hope any of my former colleagues reading this story will forgive me.

DETECTIVE EDWARD GALVAN COULDN'T HELP NOTICING THAT Anne Peabody kept glancing back at the chair where she'd found her boss's body. "I -- I came in here for an early meeting -- " Glance. " -- and I said 'hi,' and he didn't turn around. I said it again -- " Glance. " -- and he still didn't -- " She clapped her hand to her mouth and fought to suppress tears. Her shoulders shook. "I'm sorry, I -- I've been to dozens of crime scenes back when I was a reporter, but when it's someone you know . . . "

"I understand," Galvan said as he recalled one of his personal guidelines: The person who discovers the body is often the prime suspect.

The body of Matthew Kristol, who had served as the General Manager of Local News Now, a local cable channel, had already been taken away after the Medical Examiner made a preliminary determination of what appeared self-evident: cause of death was the bullet wound directly in Kristol's face. Now CSI Katie Melendez was busy scouring the office for potential evidence. Working her magic, was how Galvan thought of it.

He also hoped that her magic, and any he might conjure, could close this case quickly. *Even involving a relatively small media outlet like this one,* he thought, *this could end up being a lot more high-profile than I'd like. We've already got plenty of uniforms both outside and inside the facility. Plenty of flashing red and blue lights. Soon we could have big brass on the scene, lots of attention. I'd like to avoid that.*

Peabody was the channel's News Director. She told Galvan, "I swear I didn't touch anything. And I called it in the moment I found him."

"We appreciate that," Galvan said. "It's barely eight-fifteen now. What time was your meeting?"

"Seven. Roger was usually the first person here, other than our overnight people. He liked getting an early start. I was here right on time, and found him there."

"Who else would've been here?"

"Just our morning anchor, Roger Borders. Overnight Maintenance Engineer Ricky Tomlinson. And Master Control Operator Lydia Philpot."

"What does she do?" Galvan asked.

"Runs all the commercials. Punches up the production control room for the news cut-ins."

"I see. Should anyone else have come in here since you found the body?"

Peabody told Galvan, "Some of the sales people make it

in by eight. We have more news personnel who arrive by nine."

"What kind of surveillance cameras do you have?"

"One at each entrance. None inside."

"At some point, we'll need to take a look at the recordings, make sure no one's been here who shouldn't have been."

"Of course," Peabody said. "You can also ask Lydia. She sees all the cameras from her position in Master Control."

If we can trust her word, Galvan thought, but told Peabody, "I'll be sure to do that." He looked past Peabody and saw Katie Melendez trying to catch his eye. "If you'll excuse me," he told Anne Peabody, "I'll need you to show me around in just a minute."

"Certainly."

Galvan entered the dead man's office. He asked Katie, "What'a ya got?"

Katie held up a plastic evidence bag containing a pistol. "Nine millimeter. Pretty common. Wiped clean."

"Anything else?"

"Not just yet. I'll let you know. Did you hear what the M.E. said about where Kristol was shot?"

"Yeah," Galvan said. "Right in the face, at close range. Sounds personal."

Katie said, "I'll let you know if I find out anything else here. Especially since I see that expression on your face."

"What expression's that?"

"The trying-to-make-an-arrest-before-the-big-shots-get-here face," Katie said.

"Don't you want that, too?"

"Sure I do. Don't be contrary."

"Too late," Galvan said, and went back to Anne Peabody, saying, "Let's go see Lydia Philpot."

PEABODY LED GALVAN DOWN A SHORT STRETCH OF CORRIDOR, with some doors along the way leading into rather normal-looking offices, others to larger rooms filled with plenty of broadcast tech. The quick peeks he made into such areas told him he didn't understand what a bit of it was for.

When they entered Master Control, Galvan found himself in a cramped room surrounded by even more tech -- plenty of banks of monitors, buttons, switches, flashing lights, and other devices he didn't even know how to describe. At one end of the room sat a woman with a finger poised over one of several rows of buttons. On the largest monitor before her, a national news anchor Galvan thought he recognized wrapped up a segment, and as the screen was about to go dark, the woman punched the button and a local anchor, presumably Roger Borders, a man who appeared to be in his early sixties, began to read.

Peabody explained, "So what you saw was that the national news tossed to us locally. What Lydia did there was punch up our own production control on the air."

"So, production control is where the newscast is actually produced?"

Peabody drew in a breath through clenched teeth. "Well, it's not much of a production. Roger's kind of a one-man-band. Points the camera, goes in front of it and reads the news. No video, no graphics. It's five minutes of content with two minutes of commercials in the middle. Nothing like our midday and evening newscasts, and quite honestly it's embarrassing, a holdover from previous owners. But that's going to change soon."

"How's that?"

"We're about to expand these cut-ins to four full hours of

news from five until nine in the morning. Full production crew, full news staff. An expensive proposition, but even on a cable station like this one, we have to do it to compete with the broadcast stations."

"I think I understand," Galvan said. Borders tossed to a commercial, which Lydia Philpot played as Galvan watched.

Anne Peabody pointed to a smaller black-and-white monitor next to the larger color one. "See that camera shot? Where we've been watching Roger read the news?"

"The camera's moving now."

"Roger's moving it over to the weather board. He's got two minutes to get there and frame up his own shot."

"This all seems rather makeshift."

Peabody sighed. "Like I said before, embarrassing is what it is."

The commercial ended and Lydia rejoined the studio feed. Galvan said to her, "Could I ask a couple of questions right now?"

The woman turned and offered her hand to shake. "Lydia Philpot."

"Detective Edward Galvan. Pleased to meet you, though sorry for the circumstances."

"Circumstances?"

"You don't know? Your General Manager Matthew Kristol's been shot."

"Shot? Damn! How is he? Is he . . . ?"

"I'm afraid he's dead. Shot in his office."

Anne Peabody said, "I wanted to wait until we knew something more before I told any of the staff."

"Oh, no," Philpot said. "That's what that sound was."

Galvan asked, "What sound?"

"I must've heard the gunshot. I didn't know what it was, and I was right in the middle of the six fifty-five cut-in. But if it happened in his office, I guess that's what I heard."

"So what time was that?"

"I looked right at our master clock. Six fifty-seven thirty-two."

Anne Peabody gasped. "That means I just -- just missed the shooter."

Galvan asked Philpot, "Did you see anyone come in this morning who wouldn't normally be here?"

"Just me, and Roger of course. And Ricky, the overnight maintenance tech."

"So as far as you know, no one's here who shouldn't be."

"I'd know. A pretty loud bell rings when any of the doors open. When you sit here pretty much by yourself overnight, you get kinda paranoid hearing that bell. And no one's left, either." Philpot turned back to her console. "Hold on just a moment. Gotta rejoin network."

On the main screen, Roger Borders wrapped up his weather forecast and was mentioning the network news which was about to continue. On the screen next to the on-air monitor, Galvan saw the network anchors already speaking. The instant Borders wrapped up, Philpot joined the network. "Dammit," she said. "He upcut network again. By four seconds this time."

Galvan asked, "What does that mean?"

Anne Peabody said, "It means he didn't finish before the network people started. He's supposed to keep an eye on the clock and shut up in time."

Philpot said, "At least he did a little better this time. He did the same thing during that six fifty-five cut-in, only it was six seconds."

"So that's why we caught the network people in the middle of a sentence."

Philpot told him, "They have a couple hundred affiliates that air them. They can't wait for all of us to finish. We have to conform to their timing."

"I get it. So forgive me for the question, Ms. Philpot. It looks as if both you and Mr. Borders would've been pretty busy at the moment of the shooting."

Philpot scrunched up her face. "If you're thinking of either of us as possible suspects, you can forget the whole thing. Neither one of us would have time to get away with that. In fact, Roger was in the studio quite a while ahead of that cut-in, rehearsing."

Peabody spoke up. "And, of course, Lydia here had to roll that break in the middle."

"Pardon me for asking," Galvan said, "but could that be automated?"

"Absolutely not. We don't have that kind of equipment. At least not yet. That's something we're getting with our newscast expansion."

"I understand," Galvan said. "Now I need to speak with Mr. Borders."

"Of course. He's probably still tidying up the studio."

Galvan followed Peabody into the studio area. The first thing he noticed was the news set, the focus of the room. The anchor desk had a slight curve to it, and chairs for four people to sit. *Ah, I get it,* Galvan thought. Weather guy, two anchors, sports guy, if they're doing the evening news.

Galvan recognized Borders from his appearance on TV minutes earlier. He was positioning one of the studio cameras against a wall. Galvan went to him and offered his hand for Borders to shake. "I'm Detective Edward Galvan. I'm investigating the death of Matthew Kristol."

Borders said, "What? What? Matthew -- dead?"

Anne Peabody said, "I found the body. It happened during your six fifty-five cut-in."

Borders rubbed his chin. "My God. Who ... who did it?"

"That's what I'm trying to figure out, Mr. Borders."

"Don't worry," Peabody said. "We know you and Lydia were both busy when it happened."

Borders looked distracted. "Of course. I was . . . right here. On the air. Thousands of people saw me."

"I understand, Mr. Borders," Galvan said, then said to Peabody, "I'd like to talk to that third person. The maintenance engineer?"

———————

RICKY TOMLINSON LOOKED UP AT GALVAN AND PEABODY FROM a piece of equipment he had his right hand buried in. When Galvan introduced himself and explained that Matthew Kristol had been killed, Tomlinson said, "Then I guess I could've figured out you'd be down here eventually." He pulled his hand from the device and wiped both hands on a soiled cloth.

"How's that?" Galvan asked.

Tomlinson glared at Peabody as he said, "It's just the last straw. All we've heard about for the past few weeks are some kind of shakeup, with people being let go even though they're adding all this morning show stuff. If you ask me, just doing news at all here is a pain in the ass. Makes engineers' lives that much harder, people always wanting something and wanting it right now, right now."

Peabody said, "That's the nature of news, Ricky. We can't wait around for something to be fixed when we're about to go on the air."

Got to get things back on track, Galvan thought. "Where were you during that cut-in?"

"Right here doing just what I'm doing right now. Though of course I can't prove that. No one here to see me. "

Peabody gave Galvan a worried look, which Galvan ignored. "I'm not going to question you further right now."

Tomlinson said, "I thought you'd wanna take me downtown, Mirandize me, all that. Tell me, are you the good cop or the bad cop?"

"Ricky!" Peabody said. "There's no reason to talk like that."

Galvan said, "It's all right."

Tomlinson gave a bitter chuckle and just shook his head. He returned his attention to the broken piece of equipment. "I'm not the screw-up everyone seems to think I am. Not like Roger Borders."

Galvan asked, "What about Roger Borders?"

"I hear things. Anne, here, must hear them, too. I tuned in to that last cut-in. Where he didn't wrap in time and upcut network. When he doesn't go long, he goes short and sits there looking like a fool. He stumbles on copy all the time."

Peabody said, "That's enough, Ricky. None of that's your concern."

"Maybe not. But you and the producers and anchors seem to make it your concern if a video editor isn't working or a live truck goes down."

"Thank you, Mr. Tomlinson," Galvan said, and made his way into the corridor. Once they were out of earshot, Galvan asked Peabody, "What was that all about?"

"He's just paranoid. Ricky's a good engineer, and we have no reason to get rid of him. All the changes are happening in the news department, anyway."

"And Roger Borders? Is his performance as bad as he said it was?"

"Roger's been here a long time. Found a way to fill the gap on these morning cut-ins before the new budget kicks in."

"He seems as if he cares about what he's doing. Lydia Philpot mentioned he was rehearsing earlier."

"Which news people don't normally do. I guess it's to be commended. But, in all honesty, the corporate folks think they might replace him once the new format's established."

"Aren't you the news director? Don't you decide those things?"

"When it comes to air talent, you're going beyond purely journalistic concerns into the station's image and ratings potential. For years we've been 'The Little Channel That Could,' competing with the big broadcast stations. I think upper management might like to trade up. I'd like to keep Roger on in some capacity, but I might be overruled."

"Upper management like the late Matthew Kristol."

"Exactly." Peabody gave Galvan a hard stare. "But we already know Roger couldn't have killed him. He was on the air."

"Let's just see about that," Galvan said, and privately relished Peabody's confused expression.

ROGER BORDERS CAME TO THE DOORWAY OF THE SMALL ROOM that was packed with video editing equipment. *An edit bay, that's what they call it,* Galvan recalled. Anne Peabody stood next to him, in front of a video monitor and computer keyboard.

"Com'on in," Galvan said.

Borders hesitated a moment, then started to back away. At the sight of a uniformed officer coming down the hallway, he stopped. Blinked.

Galvan told him, "You might as well see what we have in here."

Borders stepped into the cramped room. Didn't speak, just looked at Galvan, then at Peabody.

Galvan told the news director, "Go ahead and show him."

Peabody pressed a button, and the monitor in front of her lit up with video of Borders reading the news. "I'm told these are the same stories that aired during the six fifty-five cut-in."

Borders tilted his head slightly. "What if they are? I did a rehearsal."

"Let's just keep watching."

On the video, Borders read his final story, paused a moment, then disappeared from view for a moment. The camera moved across the studio to the weather board. The shot settled down, and Borders stepped in front of the camera again.

Galvan asked Peabody, "So this business of resetting the camera would be during the commercial break."

Peabody's voice sounded as if it were about to crack. "Yes, it is."

A moment later, the video showed Borders giving the weather report. Then he promoted the network news which was coming right up. When Borders' video image stopped speaking, Galvan told Peabody, "Stop it right there."

Peabody hit a different button and the video paused.

Galvan asked, "How long is it?"

Peabody looked at a numerical readout. "Five minutes -- and six seconds."

Galvan looked at Borders. "Funny thing, huh? That six

seconds is the same amount of time that you went over into the network at the six fifty-five cut-in. At least, that's what Lydia Philpot told us."

"What does she know?" Borders muttered. "She's no better than anyone else."

"Maybe so. But when she mentioned a 'rehearsal' you did earlier, and when Ms. Peabody here told me that normally you don't do rehearsals, I added things up. I hear you're a bit of a screw-up, Mr. Borders. I was counting on that, on you not getting rid of this recording, which gave you the chance to go upstairs and kill Matthew Kristol."

"So Anne's the same as everyone else. All of them against me. Just like Matthew Kristol was."

Galvan told Borders, "Be careful what you say next, Mr. Borders."

"You're right," Borders said. "I guess I need to call my lawyer."

Galvan motioned for the uniformed officer, who cuffed Borders and took him away.

"How'd you figure that out?" Anne Peabody asked. "Everyone else just knew it couldn't be him, I didn't think it could be him."

"I've been doing this a long time," Galvan said. "Ricky Tomlinson was the obvious suspect, but that's the part I didn't like. And in listening to him, I thought I heard someone who bitches a lot but never does anything about it."

"You're right, there. He's actually one of our better employees, even though he thinks he's constantly on the verge of being fired."

"Quite honestly, I also didn't like that everyone seemed to be telling me he was the obvious suspect." Galvan shrugged. "Yeah. I guess I'm just contrary."

WRAITHS

When I read Bob Drury and Tom Clavin's book HALSEY'S TYPHOON, I was struck by the heroism and determination of the American sailors who fought to survive the destructive storm that struck the U.S. Pacific Fleet in December of 1944, during World War II. Admiral William "Bull" Halsey received inaccurate information about the direction of the typhoon, and unwittingly guided his fleet right into the middle of it. With several ships sinking, and hundreds of sailors dying, the storm's toll was compared to that of a major combat incident.

With my story sense always active, I had to wonder whether such a harrowing experience could lead someone to committing a serious crime they'd never otherwise consider.

George Adler's head and his left side slammed against the tilting wall of the *USS William Litton* as the typhoon continued to pound the destroyer. Adler shook his head, rubbed his shoulder, groaned, but kept moving down the narrow corridor as the ship tilted more precipitously to port. *We're almost at 70 degrees,* Adler thought. *Much more, and the ship will roll over.*

Admiral William Halsey, Jr's Third Pacific Fleet had expected to engage a Japanese fleet, not a force of nature.

Adler heard a sudden onrush of water behind him. It struck the backs of his knees, nearly knocking him over. *If I fall, I'm dead*, Adler thought as he stumbled over an open hatchway that was supposed to be to one side, but now yawned dangerously underfoot. Ahead of him, a sailor slipped off the deck and crashed onto the wall. *It's like being in the funhouse at Coney Island*, he thought. *Only without the fun.*

Adler recognized that sailor as Dewey Mickelson, someone he'd only seen aboard a couple of times, and one of those for a routine exam Adler had given him in his role as the ship's doctor. The man had enlisted the day after Pearl Harbor. "Com'on, Dewey," Adler said, grabbing him by the shoulders. He tilted his head to indicate the rising waters behind them. "We've got to keep moving."

Dewey found his footing and moved ahead. "Don't I know it, Doc? I can't even swim!"

Adler kept ahold of of Dewey's shoulder to steady him as the corridor ahead of them tilted up. *I don't know how fast we're going down*, Adler thought, *but it may not matter. What good will it do us to leap off a sinking ship into a typhoon?*

If Captain Thornton hadn't been an incompetent ass --

No time to think of that now, though. Time to leave.

Four more sailors, their faces and uniforms covered with soot and coal dust identifying them as part of the "black gang" who worked in the engine room, joined them at a cross-corridor, most of them wearing the newer rectangular life jackets called kapoks that had replaced the more familiar Mae West life belts. *Good for them*, Adler thought. *They disobeyed the captain's order not to put the jackets on. He didn't want to frighten the crew!*

One of the sailors, Leonard Gehr, told Adler, "Everything down below that isn't flooded is on fire. Doc, where's your kapok?"

"Don't have one yet."

"We'll find you one, Doc," Gehr said, and led the way up a ladder.

Adler was the last to make his way up the ladder. He arrived up top just ahead of the rising waters in the corridor below and stepped --

-- into utter darkness and chaos.

Waves eighty feet tall, appearing from nothingness like wraiths, hammered the *Litton*, tilting the 2000-ton destroyer at a dangerous angle; the sun seemed a distant memory. Sailors all around Adler sent up shouts of instruction or of fear, all of them drowned out in the roaring winds. A large lifeboat at the rear of the ship had disappeared, along with a stash of depth charges.

Two men were scrambling for purchase along the tilting deck, and Adler reached toward them in desperation. The tips of his fingers slid against one man's shirt, slipped away, and both sailors tumbled into the rough seas.

Adler hunkered down to gain his bearings. A hard object struck his face, and when he grasped at it, his hands were holding one of the kapok life jackets. "For you, Doc," Leonard Gehr shouted from a couple of feet away.

As Adler put on the jacket and tied it around his waist, he shouted his thanks, but Gehr was already moving away. *He doesn't even have his own kapok on*, Adler realized.

Gehr stopped cold. Pointed past Adler's shoulder. He turned.

Another ship, a cruiser, bore down upon the *Litton*, its bow aimed arrow-sharp at the destroyer's center.

It struck.

Adler's feet left the deck, whether from the collision with the cruiser or from the typhoon winds, he couldn't tell. He felt as if he were flying, not falling, as the ocean grew closer, then swallowed him up. Darkness enveloped him.

Which way's the surface? was his first desperate thought.

He chose a direction and swam for his life.

Adler's chest felt as if it would burst as his lungs demanded air. His ears popped.

He broke the water's surface as if shot from a cannon. A desperate gasp for air, then he struck the water again. *Of course*, he realized. *The kapok brought me back.* A wave twice the height of the *Litton* crashed against him, and again he soared, again he crashed.

Adler, after some struggling, found a rhythm, riding with the waves rather than fighting them. *But where's the* Litton? he wondered.

A smooth dark shape to his right appeared from the surrounding gloom, and Adler realized -- *That's the* Litton! *It's rolled over. And sinking fast.* Adler swam furiously away from the ship, fearing that at any moment he'd fell its inexorable pull carrying him back into the deeps.

Changing direction broke his rhythm with the massive waves, and the next one caught him off-guard, sending him tumbling across the waters as he took a deep breath and squinted against the onrushing water.

When he opened his eyes again, he saw dozens of indistinct forms silhouetted against the mass of metal that was the rapidly disappearing form of the *Litton*. A flash from within the ship, and a loud, low crumpling sound, and Adler realized the ship's boilers were exploding. The shock wave knocked what little breath he retained out of him, and his flight to the surface became desperate.

Arms and legs straining, lungs near bursting once again, at what Adler believed would be his final instant of life, he broke surface.

Winds roared, waves tossed him in all directions. Each breath, however short, he managed to take was a miracle. Raindrops felt like hailstones against his face.

And all because of the incompetence of Captain Thornton, he thought. His consciousness burned with a white heat at the very thought of the captain who'd refused to move out of the way of the oncoming typhoon, citing Admiral Halsey's orders to maintain the fleet's formation, which was clearly impossible.

And now the ship's gone, he thought, *who knows how many of the men aboard her are dead or dying, and how the hell is anyone supposed to rescue us or even notice us in these violent waters?*

Adler resumed his rhythm of riding with the waves, though his strength already lagged from earlier. *I've got to find something to hold onto,* he thought. *Best would be a lifeboat with other survivors, but I'd take a cargo net, a group of planks or --*

Planks! Just ahead of me!

Adler changed course, arms and legs flailing, fighting against the waves continually steering him away from the planks. *I can't even get more than the briefest glimpse of them,* he thought, every stroke a test of his remaining strength.

Then -- success! He grasped the edge of the group of planks, which was barely wide enough and long enough for him to pull himself onto. Even then, his exertions didn't end. He knew a single moment of weakness or inattention would send him flying off his perch and back into the churning ocean.

He freed a hand long enough to pat his chest and check to make sure the flashlight and whistle were still attached to his kapok. They were. *If the storm would just let up,* he thought, *maybe I've have a chance. The kapok's supposed to keep a man afloat as long as three or four days, longer than the old Mae West's.*

But what about the rest of the men? Like Dewey Mickelson? He couldn't swim. Did he ever get a life vest on? Is he still out here, or did he join so many of the other men who went down with the ship?

Adler spent several minutes developing a new rhythm to his technique of riding with the waves as he rode upon his narrow vessel of planks. For a time he might anticipate those waves as they swept him onward to an unknown destination; then that pattern would disrupt itself, and more than once he and the planks were nearly separated.

A couple of times he thought he heard the sounds of men shouting, but he never caught sight of them. *I can't be the only survivor,* he thought. *Three-hundred-something officers and men can't have just disappeared.*

But what if they have? I could be the only one left to tell the tale of what happened, to tell them all about Captain Thornton, how he froze and turned coward and --

A succession of particularly strong waves thrust such thoughts from his consciousness, as he concentrated only on keeping himself afloat, keeping alive.

Eventually Adler knew that hours must have passed, but he had no idea how many. His exertions were so vital a part of his existence that he became aware only slowly that his body neared exhaustion. He couldn't escape from the constant stinging of his eyes from saltwater. He had no idea whether it was day or night; the enveloping storm made such a distinction unknowable. The content waves shredded his clothing into rags. He felt as if he'd never known a time when his face and body hadn't been pounded with constant rain and the rhythmic tossing of the waves.

Adler fought the urge to sleep, knowing that a moment's inattention would topple him beneath the roiling waters to join the unknown number of sailors from the *Litton* whom the sea already embraced. Fought the urge and --

-- JERKED AWAKE, HIS HANDS DESPERATELY GRIPPING HIS FRAIL vessel of planks. *That could've been it*, he thought. *I could've* --

A shout from behind. He strained to turn around while maintaining his hold upon his makeshift craft.

After a moment, he saw the other sailor, fighting the waves as furiously as Adler knew he was doing, gaining on him only slowly. Every few seconds the other man would disappear behind the latest rush of waves, and Adler felt a strange, intense grief for potentially losing someone who, as far as he knew, was a stranger to him. He tried to aim his makeshift craft toward the last place he'd glimpsed the man.

There! The sailor, his lined features and straining arms and legs clearly showing that he was using his last measure of strength, grabbed onto the rear of Adler's ship of planks. Adler twisted himself around to help the man aboard.

Not a stranger after all, Adler thought, recognizing the man as Roy Pickett, a radarman from the *Litton*. Pickett wrapped him in a tight embrace, and for his part Adler grasped Pickett as he would have his own mother.

"Why, Doc," Pickett said as he released his embrace, "it's you!"

"None other," Adler said, taking Pickett's measure. *If I look anything like him,* he thought, *I'm in bad shape.* Pickett's forehead sported a big bruise, his left arm had a long deep scratch down it, and the man's clothing was as ragged as his own. At least he also wore a kapok.

"Here, let's arrange ourselves as best we can. Not a lot of room here."

As they each found handholds on the narrow stretch of boards, Adler said, "I've been trying to roll with the waves instead of fighting them. It's worked the best."

"Gotcha, Doc."

Adler worked to adapt his own rhythm to Pickett's as the unending waves carried them to -- who knew where? Adler's exertions kept him from speaking more for a time, and it was Pickett who broke the silence: "Seen anyone else since the ship sank, Doc?"

"You're the first. What about you?"

"I, uh . . . yeah, I saw one man. Can't rightly say his name. He was dead soon after. I got his dogtags before I let him sink away."

"That's tough," Adler said. I don't have any idea how many more went down with 'er. I just know I'll never forgive Captain Thornton for the way he handled things. Damn incompetent bastard."

Adler paused as they hung on tightly while traversing an especially tall wave. Then he continued: "I'd be right there to tell a court of inquiry that, too. Unless I got my hands around his neck first." He told Pickett how the captain feared that ordering the crew to put lifejackets on would frighten them, a shocking violation of normal procedure. "Better frightened than dead. And I'd bet most of the crew's learned that the hard way."

"Hey, Doc?"

"Yeah?"

"Can we talk about something else?"

"Sorry, Pickett. I know I was starting to rant. But I saw Leonard Gehr just before I got swept off the ship. He gave me this kapok. I gave him a physical just last week and he says he writes his wife every day. Piles up the letters until we hit shore somewhere he can send them off."

"I know what you mean, Doc. Everyone has their quirks. You know Benjamin Camino?"

Another massive wave came along, and Adler couldn't speak, could only hold on tight as he and Pickett rode the crest. He spit out salt water. "Ben came to me with a fever one day. Gave him some aspirin and told him to get some rest. So I didn't know him that well."

"Hah! You sure didn't. He hated being called 'Ben.' It was always 'Benjamin' for him."

Adler said, "I'd call him 'Aunt Martha' if he wanted, if we just had a chance to see him again. Him, and all the other men aboard. If only I could get my hands on Captain Thornton -- "

"Wait a minute," Pickett said, pointing ahead of them. "Look at that!"

Adler looked in the direction Pickett was pointing and saw the running lights of a distant ship. He fumbled at his chest to grab the small flashlight out of his kapok. He flashed it in the direction of the ship, and started yelling. "We're over here!" Pickett cried out as well, but it didn't look as if the ship were coming any nearer.

Finally, Adler had to admit: "It's going farther away."

"Dammit," Pickett said, "I let myself anticipate a good warm meal. And just something as simple as a good cold drink of water! I'm almost tempted to -- "

"Don't," Adler told the other man. "You know how much

the salt in seawater can harm you. You can become anemic and weak within hours, and start hallucinating."

"If we don't die of hypothermia first."

Adler looked once again in the direction of the vanished ship. "It's a big fleet. Someone will find us."

He hoped Pickett's silence implied agreement and not an unwillingness to contradict him.

———

Hours later, Adler's mind tried to tell him he'd never been anywhere but here in the middle of the Philippine sea, endlessly holding onto his makeshift raft, grasping it as if it were his own mother, fighting to ride with the constant waves, Pickett the only companion he'd ever known.

He heard his own voice, as if from a distance, say, "Mother . . ."

"What's that?" Pickett asked.

"Sorry," Adler said, the necessity of responding to Pickett bringing his consciousness back around to embrace reality. "Just thinking about my mother. I'm an only child. If I, you know, don't make it, it'll crush her. I volunteered, you know. Didn't wait for the draft. She understood, and my father said he was proud of me. He'll tough his way through losing me, but Mother will be devastated."

Pickett didn't say anything. After a moment's pause, Adler asked, "What about your family?"

The other sailor's eyes were tightly closed, and Adler didn't think it was just from the seawater. "Not much to tell."

"Listen, Pickett, I've been about to fall asleep for the last couple hours. We've got to keep talking about something, anything."

"All right, all right. I just . . . I just don't have any close family. Mom died of tuberculosis a few years before the war. My father . . . he left me with an aunt and uncle."

"Your own father -- he -- "

"Abandoned me, yes. Nothing I'm proud of."

"None of that's your fault, Pickett. And if your relatives took you in . . . "

"They did it thinking my father would take me back in a few months. Those few months turned to years. They kept telling me I was no good, that they knew I'd turn out bad like my father. They were glad when I joined up and left."

Another round of giant waves thrust them forward. Adler couldn't tell whether the moisture on his face was seawater or tears. "You've had it tough, then, Pickett. But not as tough as these other boys at the bottom of the ocean."

"We'll be there soon enough."

"Not if we hang on."

"What keeps you goin', Doc?"

"I told you one thing. My mother. I'm more worried about her than I am about myself. I guess love will do that."

Pickett squinted against the pouring seawater. "'One thing' sounds like there's another."

Adler said, "I've talked about that, too. Captain Thornton. Looks like revenge is a pretty powerful motivator, too. I looked at him just as I was about to head below decks to check on some of the men. The ship was just starting to pitch over. Thornton just stood there."

"What do you mean, 'just stood there?'"

"Exactly that. Stared ahead at the wind and the rain and the waves. Wouldn't respond when someone asked for orders or instruction. Just stood there. Didn't do a damn thing."

"But the ship was turning over!"

Adler said, "I wanted to bash the hell out of his head, but

I had to get below. I wanted to make sure some of the men got out. And I was there with some of them -- Dewey Mickelson, Leonard Gehr. I told you Gehr gave me this kapok. We helped each other get out and now who knows whether they're still alive or not. All because of Captain Thorn -- "

"Doc!" Pickett said. "Look, more lights -- it's another ship!" He fumbled for his flashlight, aimed it in the direction of the distant vessel.

Adler said, "Wait a minute." He blocked Pickett's light with one hand. "I see it. But it doesn't look like something from our fleet."

Pickett switched off the flashlight. "You're right. Looks like a sub, which means it's not one of ours. Dammit!"

"'Dammit' is right. Not a good choice ahead of us. Prisoners of war, or drowning."

The vessel drew closer. Finally, after all of these hours, the storm was abating; dim threads of sunlight shone down, giving them a better look at the approaching craft.

"Wait a minute," Adler said. "Look closer. It *is* one of ours. A destroyer, looks like. But it's taken a pounding. A lot of its superstructure's been pounded off." Adler drew out his flashlight, and he and Pickett swept their beams in the direction of the American ship. They could just make out the noise of its engines over the fading fury of the storm.

In the next moment, though, the destroyer turned away from them. "No, no, no!" Pickett said. "Why don't they see us?"

"Just wait," Adler told him. "I see what he's doing. They call it a 'boxed search.' Fifteen hundred yards on a side. She should come back in this direction in a minute or so."

Instead, the destroyer's engine noise faded and all its lights went off. "That's so they can better see and hear any survivors," Adler said. "So start yelling, and wave that flashlight!"

Adler waved his light furiously, shouted as if to be heard in Heaven. Pickett also waved his light, but blew the whistle included with the kapok rather than shouting. Just as Adler wondered which would give out first, the flashlight or his voice, the destroyer's engines spun up again, its lights illuminated, and it turned toward him and Pickett.

Adler slapped Pickett's back so hard, the other man nearly fell off their makeshift vessel of planks. The two men embraced one another in joy and relief. "I can't believe it," Adler said. "Think about it -- just like you were saying before -- a hot meal, warm bed, dry clothes. It'll be paradise."

Pickett pulled himself from Adler's grip. "A paradise I won't see," he said, sliding his legs into the still-churning waters.

Adler grasped Pickett's arm, but Pickett pulled away. "I don't understand," Alder said, indicating the ship which drew ever-closer. "We're about to be rescued!"

"And I know what'll happen then. I couldn't stand to face trial. Couldn't stand to see what's left of my family say I'd turned out as bad as my father."

"Pickett -- you're hallucinating. Get back up here -- the ship's so close."

Pickett reached into his shirt, pulled out a set of dogtags, slapped them into Adler's hand. Before Adler could look at them, though, another strong wave swept over him and he had to grasp the planks with both hands, and Pickett's arm slid from his grasp.

Pickett was floating away. He managed to make himself heard over the storm winds: "I know you'll have to tell them what happened. You see, I hated that son-of-a-bitch, too. Damn coward, he was. And when I came across him in the water I didn't want to take the chance of just letting the typhoon kill him. I held him under to make sure the job got done."

Adler remembered Pickett's words earlier: *I saw one man. Can't rightly say his name. He was dead soon after. I got his dogtags before I let him sink away.*

Pickett disappeared into nothingness like a wraith beneath the remnants of the typhoon.

Adler barely heard the shouts of the men aboard the rapidly approaching destroyer, barely responded as one sailor dove into the rough waters, secured by a rope, and hauled him aboard. His mind would only focus on the name on the dogtags he grasped desperately in his fist, the last remaining evidence that such a man lived:

THORNTON, VICTOR ALOYSIUS

Even as more sailors wrapped Adler in blankets and offered him a warm drink, his consciousness fought to decide which emotion held him more powerfully -- grief over Pickett's death, and the fact that he *would* acknowledge the man's crime to their superiors, giving his unfaithful family something to *tsk-tsk* about as they sat safe and secure on their front porches, or the regret that he'd never have the chance to confront Thornton in a court of inquiry or place his hands around that cowardly, incompetent neck and squeeze.

STARTING FROM SCRATCH

(with Dana Moore)

OK, SO HERE'S ANOTHER ONE WHERE THE INTRODUCTION threatens to be longer than the story. Suffice it to say that my wife Dana Moore had the basic idea, stemming from our mutual love of cats, and I expanded it.

CONNIE ROSS WANTED TO MAKE SURE THE MONEY WAS handled the way Mrs. Henderson would have wanted. She had to find it quickly, before someone beat her to it. Connie paused before the grand old house where her friend had lived.

Every day for six years, Connie had walked the three blocks to Mrs. Henderson's house to feed the old woman's cats. Besides being an animal lover, Connie considered her dedication a tribute to her late mother. Mrs. Henderson had been her mom's best friend all her life. Connie would spend those few minutes each day thinking about her mother--always the fond memories, the happy times. It was a simple ritual, and a peaceful one.

Each day when she arrived, Connie would wait patiently for Mrs. Henderson to get to the door. It always took a while for her to make the journey from her bedroom to the front door. Connie always smiled at the sweet old lady as she peeked through the curtains of a window next to the door. Then Mrs. Henderson had to undergo the laborious task of unfastening each bolt and chain on the door one by one.

Now Connie inserted Mrs. Henderson's spare key into the single lock that she knew would be the only one fastened. Mrs. Henderson had passed away three days earlier. This was Connie's first visit since then. Her work schedule had kept her away, and she knew even the generous helpings of food she'd left would be depleted by now.

She slipped through the door, her entry accompanied by a chorus of meows from the eleven cats that had been Mrs. Henderson's constant companions. Connie reached down to pet the most persistent of the mini-mob surrounding her legs. She knew they must be hungry.

She nodded knowingly when she saw the kitchen. Only random bits of the dry cat food she'd left out in the half-dozen cat bowls remained uneaten. And the kitty litter boxes reeked. "All right, everyone," Connie said. "I'd better get you all fed first. She knew none of the felines would leave her alone until their needs were taken care of.

Connie opened several cans of cat food--which they liked much better than the dry stuff--and served the crying kitties. She checked to make sure the kitchen faucet was still dripping steadily--the cats liked their water fresh. The litter boxes would have to wait, and it was an unaccustomed duty she wasn't eager to tackle anyway. Mrs. Henderson would never let her change the litter, saying it was one chore she would never wish on another. Besides, Connie was too eager to start her search for the money.

It was eerie to rummage through the house without Mrs. Henderson present. She'd feared that accepting this responsibility, and having to be all alone in this empty house, would overwhelm her. But this was something she'd started, and she knew she had to finish it.

A lot was riding on whether she could find that money. It was over a quarter of a million dollars. At least that's what Mrs. Henderson confided to Connie once. Mrs. Henderson always used to tell her--it wasn't a phrase her generation would have used--"Well, Connie," the sweet old woman would say, laughing, "a quarter of a million dollars is a lot of scratch."

Mrs. Henderson had left a provision in her will that part of her money would go toward the care and feeding of her cats. They were her surrogate children, and she only trusted banks so far. The rest of the cash hidden in her house was to go to the Salvation Army's homeless shelter--if it was really in the house, and if she could find it.

Where could it be?

She started in the dining room. It was filled with faded tapestry chairs and dusty shelves lined with knick-knacks. An orange tabby who had either finished eating or was more lonesome than hungry rubbed her ankles, as if providing Connie reassurance in her quest.

As soon as she found the money, Connie's next mission would be to find a home for that orange tabby and the other cats. She'd probably take a couple of them home. Dad wouldn't object. Besides, Mrs. Henderson would've been heartbroken if she'd thought a single one of her babies might have ended up in the pound.

After finding nothing in the living room, she headed for the upstairs bedroom. Finding the money stuffed into a mattress was a cliche but, Connie realized, you never know. Still, detectives had searched the house and come up empty.

At the top of the stairs, she entered the musty Victorian bedroom. The quilt and sheets were tucked in nice and neat as she'd left them four days earlier. Poor thing--it had been such an ordeal for her to climb those steps each night. But that's how she was--unwilling to accept that she was growing older, that she might have to slow down the least little bit.

Connie shook her head in wonder. Imagine passing on at the ripe old age of 98 without children or close relatives. And all that money from her stock in that silver mine. You could have called Mrs. Henderson eccentric, Connie supposed, but the money was enough to help a lot of people who might not otherwise get it. Not to mention big enough grants to keep the kitties rolling in caviar.

Nothing in the mattress. Nor did she discover anything in the dresser drawers or the closets.

The money had to be somewhere safe, but a place that was easily accessible, so it would be found easily.

Perhaps, Connie mused, she would do better just working in the house awhile, hoping for an idea to come to her on its own. Meanwhile, it was time to quit putting off an unpleasant chore. She went back downstairs.

All the cats had finished consuming their tuna and liver cat food ravenously from their half-dozen bowls on the floor of the tiny kitchen. Connie entered an alcove containing the kitty litter boxes. Six were lined up there, and Connie stood over them a long moment holding the plastic scooper in her hand, then took a deep breath and went to work.

In those first moments Connie just wrinkled her nose at the task. Then she stopped short and her eyes widened. Inside the first litter box she'd begun to clean were neatly-wrapped stacks of bills enclosed in heavy plastic bags.

She opened one of the packages -- they were filled with stacks and stacks of hundred-dollar bills. No wonder Mrs. Henderson wouldn't let anyone else change the litter! A quick survey of the other five litter boxes -- all of them were stuffed with packages of bills! Connie realized only someone who cared about the cats would ever have found the money. Mrs. Henderson had to know that would be her. Connie clutched the packages of bills to her chest, holding them closely not for their intrinsic worth but as a remembrance of Mrs. Henderson. Knowing the old lady trusted her so was worth more than anything this money could buy!

Connie chuckled aloud as she realized this explained Mrs. Henderson's old phrase: in this case, a quarter of a million dollars really was "a lot of scratch."

THE EXTRAS

A MYSTERIOUS DEATH LEAVES ONE COUPLE PONDERING HOW you might never be aware of the secrets your next-door neighbor's home may hold.

THE POUNDING ON THE FRONT DOOR SOUNDED SO LOUD AND forceful that Teresa Overdale almost wished she and her husband Ken kept a gun in the house. The only one they owned was outside in their R.V. *I've never wanted one in here,* she thought, *but I might find it a comfort right now.*

As she shook Ken's shoulder (he was a sound sleeper), she saw the flashing blue-and-red lights of a police car shining against their bedroom shades. "Com'on," she told Ken. "The police are here."

Ken rose on one elbow. "Damn. Do you think -- "

"Don't think anything," Teresa said. "Just get up."

As Teresa put on a robe and house slippers, she looked at the clock on her nightstand. Five in the morning. And she and Ken had only gotten back to sleep a few hours earlier after a disturbance that woke them up. She made her way gingerly down the narrow staircase to the entrance hall, Ken right behind her.

As Teresa turned the deadbolt to the front door, she made out the silhouettes of two officers on their front porch. One was raising his hand to pound on the door again just as she opened it. His arm paused in mid-air.

The officer was a tall African American. As he lowered his hand, Teresa couldn't help but notice that his other hand sat on top of his service weapon. *A Glock, I think they call it*, Teresa thought. The nameplate on his left breast indicated the officer's name: "Robinson." The other officer, a slender white man, was staring not at her or Ken, but at the house next door, where Harry and Julia Golden lived.

"Sorry to bother you, Ma'am," Officer Robinson said. "But your next door neighbor Mr. Golden's been in an accident, and we haven't been able to get anyone at his home to answer. Do you know if Mrs. Golden is in?"

"Oh, goodness," Teresa said. Behind the officers, the rain whose sound had acted as white noise that had helped lull her back to sleep was just letting up. The wet street in front of their house shone blue, red, and white as it reflected the police car's light bar and headlights. "I don't see why she shouldn't be. She works at home. He's an assembler at the factory just outside of town. Neither one of them normally stay out late. They're early risers, not like us. But then, we're retired."

"Have you ever heard anything unusual from over there?"

"What do you mean by unusual?" Teresa said, trying to keep her features as still as possible.

"Anything at all," Officer Robinson said. "Hear them

yelling at each other, any kind of disturbances, that sort of thing?"

Teresa fought to ignore her rapidly-beating heart, was grateful that she was unlikely to break out into a sweat in the chill air. "No, sir."

Behind her, Ken asked, "What happened to Harry?"

Officer Robinson said, "His car went off the road on the Greenwood Freeway a few hours ago."

Teresa put her hand over her mouth. "Oh, no!" That road was only two lanes, with many curves, and Teresa knew it could be tricky negotiating it even on dry pavement in the daytime. At night, on a wet, slippery road -- She asked, "So -- so how's Harry?"

The other officer, his nameplate identifying him as "Stewart," spoke up: "We can't really say right now, Ma'am."

That means he's dead, Teresa thought.

More flashing lights caught her eye -- these were red and yellow and belonged to a fire engine just coming around the corner. No siren.

Officer Stewart nodded toward Officer Robinson, who tipped his hat toward Teresa. "Excuse us, Ma'am." The two of them went across their front lawn and past the large R.V. in their driveway to meet the firefighters deploying from the fire engine.

"I wonder what that's about," Ken said. "There's no fire."

Teresa indicated a couple of the firefighters approaching the Goldens' home. "They've got one of those cute little battering rams." She stepped out onto the front porch to view the process. Both firefighters grasped the battering ram and slammed it against the Goldens' wooden front door. And again!

The third time splintered the door at the lock assembly and it burst open. One of the firefighters lowered the battering ram just inside the doorway, Teresa assumed, to hold the door open. The firefighters, though, stepped aside as Officers Robinson and Stewart entered the home. Teresa could hear their voices echoing within:

"Mrs. Golden? Are you all right?"

"Mrs. Golden, can you answer us?"

"Julia, are you OK?"

All remained quiet for several minutes. Ken leaned in close to Teresa. "Maybe those really were shots that woke us up."

"*Shh!*" Teresa responded. "Here come the Salazars." Teresa waved at Juan and Rita, their neighbors on the opposite side of their house, as they came around their shared front fence and into Teresa and Ken's yard. Juan gathered his robe together more securely as he said, "All the lights woke us up. What's going on?"

As Ken explained, Teresa moved next to Rita. She didn't say anything, just offered a sympathetic smile and held her hand for a moment.

"It's sad," Juan said. "A nice neighborhood, quiet, almost rural. Good neighbors, like the Goldens and the two of you. Then something like this. Just like ... well ... "

Teresa nodded understanding. She knew Rita had to be thinking about her and Juan's son Victor, who'd been killed in a robbery attempt two years earlier at the convenience store where he'd worked. Despite surveillance video, despite all the other evidence gathered from the crime scene, the case had never been solved. Teresa kept herself from glancing at the broad field behind her and Ken's house.

Juan asked Ken, "Did the officers tell you anything? I thought, being a retired officer yourself . . . ."

Ken shook his head. "Not my department. I don't know any of these guys."

Within moments, Teresa heard the cry of an approaching ambulance. It stopped behind the fire engine and two medical technicians carried their equipment into the Goldens' house. Soon the evidence technician unit arrived. And after that, the med-techs left, taking their equipment back to the ambulance.

"Uh, oh," Teresa said. "You don't think -- "

Her uncompleted question was answered as the ambulance pulled away, making way for a vehicle with the county coroner's logo on its side. Teresa shared a knowing glance with Ken, telling him, "We might as well go on inside and try to get a little sleep."

"I think you're right," Juan said. He and Rita started back toward their house.

"Besides," Ken said, "I have no desire to wait around to see a dead body come out."

Teresa said, "That, plus, we probably won't be able to get any work done today out back. Or at least, we shouldn't."

"You got that right," Ken said, leading the way back into the house.

THE NEXT DAY, THERE WAS NO OFFICIAL ACTIVITY AT THE Golden residence, and Teresa and Ken decided the risk was minimal and they went to work in the field that stretched several hundred feet behind their home. After a few hours of toil, they called it a day. Soon Teresa was trudging over a small rise, carrying a couple of rakes, Ken close behind her. He was pushing a wheelbarrow with two shovels and two large, empty plastic bags inside.

As they neared their house, Rita came to the back fence and motioned for Teresa to come over to her.

"I'll take the rakes," Ken said. Rita handed them over and went to the wooden fence. "My goodness," Rita said, looking at Teresa's clothing. "You've been busy -- got yourself dirty, I see."

Teresa looked down at the old jeans and a ratty t-shirt she always wore when she worked. "We've been doing some landscaping out back, just planting some shrubs. We're thinking of putting in some small trees."

"How tired you look. You and Ken should slow down some."

Teresa smiled. "Better busy than bored, I guess."

Rita leaned her arms against the fence. "Did you see the news? About what happened with the Goldens? I saw it all on the computer."

Teresa said, "I worked with computers for too long at the research agency. I try to stay off ours, on a lot of days."

Rita spoke in hushed tones, as if conveying a secret: "They found Julia's body in the house. They think Harry killed her. Shot her once in the head. Must've died instantly."

"But then what happened to Harry?"

"They say after he shot Julia, he just took off in his car. Two in the morning, dark, wet, and rainy. He didn't make that one sharp turn on the Greenwood Freeway. Hit a tree, the driver's side was smashed in, then the car went into a ditch. They found a gun that had been fired in the car. Turns out it matched the bullets that . . . you know."

"I hate to put it this way," Teresa said, "because Harry always seemed nice enough to us. But I guess he deserved it."

Rita lowered her head. "At least one murderer got what he deserved."

Teresa felt herself flush. "I'm sorry," she said, taking Rita's hands in both of her own. "I didn't -- "

A forced smile from Rita. "It's all right." She pointed to Teresa and Ken's R.V. next to their house. "Do you and Ken have any more trips planned?"

Teresa, though grateful for the change in topic, still had to work to keep her voice even. "Oh, I imagine sometime. We don't have a particular destination in mind right now."

"I saw some workers installing something new in it last week -- thought maybe you were upgrading."

Teresa let out the breath she hadn't realized she was holding. "Just a new freezer. Something a lot bigger for those long trips."

Rita's smile grew larger, more genuine. "I don't want to presume, but perhaps Juan and I could go on one of your trips sometime. We'd help pay for gas and food and anything else we'd need."

"Actually," Teresa said, "that would be great. I'm sure Ken would love the idea, too. Listen, we have to go to the store to get some supplies. I'll talk to him about it on the way."

Rita waggled her fingers at Teresa. "Thanks -- it would mean so much."

WHILE TERESA DROVE THEIR OLD, BEAT-UP PICKUP TRUCK toward their regular home improvement store, she stole glances at Ken. He sat slumped in his seat, eyes slitted, hands folded in his lap. "You look tired," she said. Of course, Rita told me *I* looked tired, too."

"Hmm," was all Ken said at first. A moment later, though, he said, "Getting that trench digger should help."

Teresa checked the rear mirror and both side ones

before she spoke: "Shouldn't we just rent one? Buying it -- I don't know. Will we get that much use out of it?" She stole another glance at Ken, who was looking straight ahead.

"I don't know," he said. "Depends on how long we keep coming back from our trips with an 'extra.'"

THEIR SHOPPING TRIP DIDN'T TAKE LONG. THEY DECIDED TO rent the trench digger instead of buying one. A store employee helped them load it and the other supplies they'd bought.

Teresa also drove on the trip back toward home. She said, "I'm glad we had the help loading up. I have to admit, those bags of material are getting heavier."

Ken smiled wanly. "Funny how we talk about 'material' and 'extras' even when we're by ourselves."

"Can't be too careful," Teresa said. "But maybe it *is* time to make a couple final trips, then lay it to rest. So to speak."

"*Then* what would we do with ourselves?"

Teresa kept her eyes on the road. "What other retired people do. Make trips just for fun. You know, Rita and Juan want to go along with us sometime. We could make a 'regular' trip with them sometime, even before we quit our special ones."

Ken said, "That could be OK. I like them. I just wish we could've . . . "

"I know. But we have to be satisfied with what we *have* done."

The death of Juan and Rita's son Victor had led Teresa and Ken to their post-retirement profession. It was the first case they'd tried to solve, but without success. They also came to fear that working locally could give them away, so they turned their attention to other cases, in Victor's memory. Though they could never tell Juan or Rita.

Teresa couldn't help but think back sometimes to the bodies in back of their house, over that rise. How many were there now? Seven? Eight? There was the child molester in Iowa, the man in Arizona embezzling from the elderly, the man who'd strangled his wife, sister-in-law, and his mother. *Made Harry Golden look like an amateur*, she thought.

Well, I guess every retiree has to find something to do in their spare time. Between Ken's police knowledge and my computer skills, and the unwillingness of some agencies to pursue cold cases, we've done well for ourselves.

Which was also why they'd invested so much of their money in the large bags of quicklime, to keep the bodies from smelling or spreading disease. Why they needed the ditch digger to make burial easier. And the new freezer in the R.V. to better preserve the individual bodies (or as they referred to them, the "extras") they'd gathered from three or four different states by now.

Ken said, "I have to admit, that business with the Goldens was a close call. I didn't like all those police around. Even with them looking at a crime that had nothing to do with us."

"They had no reason to suspect us of anything."

"I know. But part of me wishes we'd called them about the constant yelling and screaming. Maybe Julia would still be alive. I had no idea Harry would take things that far."

"Well," Teresa said as she turned into the driveway of their home, "I guess you just never know with some people."

THE CLEAT

THE INCIDENT WITH THE FLAGPOLE IN THIS STORY ACTUALLY happened to a friend from my childhood, though it was purely an accident, with no crime element. But the image stayed in my mind all those decades, until I realized that giving that incident a twist would create an interesting character drama.

———

THE MOMENT BILLY MAPLE WALKED INTO THE VINTAGE 60S diner on the outskirts of Nashville, my mind flashed back to an image from 31 years ago I'd tried to suppress -- Billy's torn and bloody body lying on the concrete in front of the neighborhood post office.

I was sitting at the counter waiting for a carry-out order. I hadn't seen Billy since those days back in high school, but he was one of those people whose basic look hadn't changed. I immediately recognized his thick blondish hair with only strands of gray, blue eyes with a greenish tint, and a walk that somehow was both loping and purposeful.

I wondered whether to turn away, but in the next instant saw the dawn of recognition on his features as he started toward me. I made myself smile as he approached, but I didn't put my hand out to shake until he extended his toward me.

His grip was solid, firm. "Well, Alex Younger! It's been a long time."

I fought for words, managed, "It has, at that, Billy."

"Actually, I prefer 'William' these days."

I gave him a nod. "'William,' then." I chanced a glance at his forehead. The only visible scar, from 31 years earlier, was faded now. You had to know it was there to see it.

But what's his chest look like after all these years? I wondered. *I can't imagine an instance where I'd get to see it. Or where I could work up the nerve to ask about it.*

Billy (I'd never be able to stop thinking of him by that name) leaned against the stool next to mine, his back to the counter. "So what're you doing these days?"

I glanced toward the kitchen to see if my food was coming up. "I'm a teacher. Elementary school."

"Just couldn't stay out of the classroom, huh?"

"I guess not."

"Married?"

"No."

"Just never found the right girl?"

"Or the time," I said.

"Time? Teachers have summers off, spring break, Christmas break . . ."

"I do a lot of charity work in my off times. It's very satisfying."

Billy tilted his head. "Oh, yeah? What kind?"

"Oh, you know, taking food to veterans over holidays. Helping build houses in the summer." Even as Billy's eyes narrowed and his mouth opened in what I knew would be a skeptical retort, I asked, "How about you?"

"Meeting my family here. Just got off work."

Family. Work. I never knew what had become of Billy, only that he'd lived. It was a relief when my family moved away just a few weeks later. Billy wasn't even out of the hospital yet. "I guess things have changed for all of us -- you know, since high school." *Since you tore your chest open -- all because I --* I asked him, "How big's your family?"

"Just me and Candy, and the kids."

"Wait a minute -- you mean you actually married Candy Raymond?"

"You don't have to sound quite that surprised! But yeah, just out of college. Two kids, Sally and Richie." Billy chuckled. "I still call them 'kids,' but they're both out of college. Sally's engaged to a guy she went to school with. And, uh, so's Richie. Engaged to a guy, that is." Billy stared me down, as if challenging me to make a smart remark.

Instead, my smile this time was sincere. "Yeah, things have changed since we were in school."

"They're both good kids," Billy said. "Never got in serious trouble once. Well, I had to pick Richie up from a party when he drank too much one night. But I'd always told him as long as he called for me, I'd never give him hell about it."

"That's the way to handle it," I ventured.

"They weren't like me," Billy said.

My heart beat faster as I anticipated where the conversation might lead, and I wondered if it was possible to suppress the urge to sweat. "You weren't so bad," I said.

"Liar!" Billy said. "I shoplifted a few things. Nothing I ever actually needed, of course. Took my dad's car a few times." He waggled a finger at me. "Now *you*, you were the good one. My dad always compared me to you. And not favorably."

A woman behind the counter plopped down a bag of food and a tall paper cup of cola. "Eight-twenty-seven, sir," she said. I handed over a ten. I told Billy, "I gotta confess something." *Though not the one thing I know, as well as I know anything, that I should confess to.*

"What's that?"

"You were kind of a hero to me. You did things I never would've dreamed of doing. Exciting things. And you got away with them."

A crooked smile from Billy. "Mostly. I was a fast talker. Got more than a few charges dropped. Or just got probation. Had to be a good boy for a little while."

Billy had no idea how much I yearned for a hopeful answer from him when I said, "Well, it sounds as if things have turned out pretty well for you." *His chest ripped open, blood pooling beneath him.*

I pulled the bag of food onto my lap, meaning to slide off the stool and leave, when Billy said, "Seeing you, Alex -- it brings up some memories I'd as soon forget, quite honestly."

Hearing those words made me stop cold -- the entire incident I'd spent most of my life trying to forget rushed into the forefront of my mind, all in a flash --

Billy shimmying up the flagpole of our neighborhood post office. He'd get to the top, jump around, and wave his arms around, especially if girls were watching. And with his bad-boy reputation in high school, there were always a few girls attracted to that.

I'd often be standing beside him, but I always used a ladder at the back of the post office building.

The girls never noticed me.

Then Billy would grasp the rope the flag attached to, pull the slack toward himself, and launch himself off the roof. Many of the girls who hadn't seen his stunt would scream; sometimes even those who had seen it.

But on the way down, he'd always grasp the actual flagpole, not counting on the rope alone to hold him.

Billy continued: "There was one memory in particular -- "

One thing I'd never told Billy -- as much as he was a hero to me, I also resented him. He was a bad kid, but he usually got away with it. Got stinking drunk with only a talking-to from his dad. I'd have been grounded forever. Got away with skipping classes and not turning in papers at school and still managing to smirk behind a teacher's back or tell us afterwards what an idiot the principal was.

" -- I'm sure it's a big memory for you, too, Alex -- "

So that one night, without even thinking, standing behind Billy where no one on the ground could see me, just as Billy was about to launch himself off that roof to the usual screams of approval, I stepped on that rope, stepped on the slack.

Here was my scenario -- Billy might smack himself against the side of the building, bruise his face or even break an arm. The screams would stop, and maybe he wouldn't be the center of attention for awhile.

Instead, Billy still managed to grasp the flagpole, but too closely, impaling his chest on the cleat -- the part of the pole the rope ties around, a word I didn't even know at the time.

The girls screamed, but this time from fright rather than excitement as the cleat ripped into Billy's flesh from his stomach to between his collarbones, then he struck the ground, hard, and the blood began to pool beneath him.

I was never happier than the day just a week later, with Billy still in the hospital, that my dad got a new job and we moved out of town. I never saw him since, never confessed to what I'd done.

"Alex -- are you listening?"

I forced my attention back to the present. "Yeah, sorry. Of course I was."

Billy ran his finger up the front of his shirt. "I was never prouder than anything than I was of this scar," he said. "Because it showed me how I had to change. How one moment of screwing up, of thinking I was hot shit, literally knocked me out of the sky. I changed. You were gone, you never saw it. I have a wonderful family, a successful business, and everything's worked out for me."

I fought to keep my breathing still. What a relief!

Though a nagging part of me wanted to confess, wanted to let Billy know just how sorry I was, that even though everything in his life had worked out for him, that I knew I'd caused him untold pain, had nearly killed him.

Billy turned toward the counter, pulled a couple of napkins from a dispenser, and handed them to me. "Looks like you need these."

I became aware of the cold sweat on my forehead. Took the napkins and wiped it off.

Felt a stinging heat on my leg. I lifted the to-go bag stuffed with of hot burgers and fries.

I couldn't make myself look at Billy. "You . . . you know I . . ."

Billy slapped my shoulder. "Alex, I know as much as I need to. I married Candy and we had Sally and Richie. By then, I had my own roofing company, and it's pretty successful to this day. Guess I turned myself around, all because of that one night."

I wadded the sweat-soaked napkins into a tight ball. I said, "I suppose that's all either of us needs to know." I gave Billy a nod, which he returned, and slid off my stool, eager to put this encounter behind me. At the door, though, I couldn't help but look back at Billy.

He smiled and, again, ran a finger from his stomach upward to his collarbones.

And winked.

OUTRACE THE SNOWFALL

THE TEMPTATION OF FINDING A VARIATION OF THE CLASSIC trope of placing a set of characters on top of a mountain, then snowing them in, was just too much for me to resist. I knew I had to make the characters compelling enough to carry the narrative and tell this kind of story in a new way. Apparently the editor at MYSTERY WEEKLY agreed, and snapped this story right up.

THE ENTIRE TRIP STARTED OFF ON SHAKY GROUND. OR AT least, slippery ground. Even a billionaire can't change the laws of physics, and our SUV, even with its four-wheel drive working as valiantly as it could, kept sliding back and forth in the darkness as it made its way up the steep, snow-covered slope to Alfred Fanning's mountain mansion. The vehicle's wipers swept across the windshield as if possessed, but to little effect as whistling winds thrust snowfall directly at us.

One skid came upon us so quickly that Dr. Richard Lin,

Alfred's personal physician, who was driving, spun the steering wheel violently to the left to correct, sending my head crashing against the right rear window where I sat. "Com'on, Richard, watch what you're doing," I said.

"Sorry, Lucy," he said. "But I can barely make out the center of the road."

Alfred, sitting in the forward passenger seat, looked back at me. His narrow eyes glared in my direction and he pointed a wrinkled finger at me. "My dear woman," he said, "please calm down. I trust Richard's driving implicitly. And I certainly have more to lose than you do."

I bit back a sharp response, hating myself as I did so. Alfred Fanning, at ninety-two years of age, held the reins of numerous investment firms, consulting agencies, and manufacturers, many of them intertwined legally and financially, and perhaps not always in ways that were legal or moral. Such wealth gave him power that extended across continents, made political philosophies irrelevant, and affected all his personal relationships right down to the four of us in this SUV. I wanted to scream at him for his condescending attitude, and demand to know what gave him the right to have such an attitude toward me, to consider himself better than me.

But I knew what gave him that right.

Money.

Money which I needed.

Eric Nussbaum, Alfred's personal chef, who shared the backseat with me, tried to favor me with a grin. I ignored him. He was a creep who wouldn't keep his hands off my ass no matter how many times I slapped those hands away.

Even Alfred's money wouldn't have led me to forgive that kind of behavior from him, and Eric didn't have anywhere near that much money.

Finally the exterior lights of the mansion shone through the snowfall, at first appearing as faint yellow smudges seemingly floating in mid-air, two lines of them, delineating the outline of the two-story stone-and-wood structure. As our vehicle drew nearer, pristine snow crunching beneath our wheels, the mansion focused into sharp relief.

We're here, I thought. *Now I have to wonder how we'll ever get back down this mountain.* Alfred had acknowledged the forecast was bad before we even left for this Montana retreat, but insisted upon making this trip anyway. And he was the boss. But I'd seen enough horror movies that I felt like kicking myself for agreeing to come along into this inaccessible wilderness. Especially as the only woman present.

As I opened my door, I squinted against the onslaught of tiny snowflakes striking my face, needle-sharp. Not fun, in contrast to how I loved playing in the snow when I was a kid. The second memory that usually occurs to me regarding a cousin, Danny, when we were seven years old, is from a family reunion on a farm and how we ran up and down a beautiful snowy landscape that made me think I was inside a picture book. We ran down to a pond that wasn't yet frozen over, and Danny showed me how to skip rocks across the water.

I wouldn't make those kind of memories this day. I stepped gingerly to the rear of the SUV as Richard opened the rear hatch and handed me my suitcase and bag. "Thanks," I muttered. Of the three men I'd be spending this no-doubt interminable weekend with, he was the least objectionable.

As I made my way around our vehicle, Alfred was scooting around out of his seat, his short legs not quite reaching the snowy ground. His wrinkled face scrunched up with concern. "Would you help me please, my dear?" he asked. "I wouldn't want to slip and fall."

Of course not, I thought, *especially since you have "so much more to lose" than I do.*

"Certainly, sir," I said. I hiked the strap of my bag up higher on one shoulder, and grasped my suitcase in one hand and grasped his arm with the other.

"Now, my dear," he said, "you know I never insist upon this 'sir' business. Makes me feel too damn old."

And would spoil your fake "everyman" image, too, I thought. Even through his thick coat, Alfred's arm felt skeletal, and it was difficult to figure out from one moment to the next how to hold onto him. Too hard and I feared bruising him or even breaking his arm. Too loose, and he could tumble right down on the ground and break a hip, or worse.

Richard rushed ahead of us to unlock the door to the mountain retreat. A thin layer of snow sat on top of the many stones that made up the main structure of the building, and covered the exterior of most of the broad windows. A large snowdrift had piled up against one side of the mansion.

Alfred and I weren't quite beneath the overhang that extended over the front entrance when I heard a sudden *swooshing* noise that I recognized as a layer of snow slipping off the roof.

"Watch out!" I said as I stepped between the onrushing mass of snow and Alfred's body.

The initial impact wasn't that hard, but the snow kept coming for three or four more seconds, pounding me on the back the entire time. By the time it stopped, Richard came up next to me and Alfred, his voice laced with concern. "Are you both all right?"

I'd grasped both of Alfred's arms and held him close to

me without even being aware of it. "I think I'm OK," I said. I stepped away from my billionaire boss, embarrassed after the fact to have been in such proximity. "Alfred?"I asked. "You all right?"

Alfred looked up at me -- at five-nine I'm a bit tall for a woman, but I had at least two inches on him -- and said, "I'm fine, my dear. I appreciate your care and attention."

I could only manage to say, "You're welcome." I certainly wasn't about to tell him I'd done that without thinking, as I would for any elderly man in imminent danger. It still didn't mean I relished being stuck up here with him. All he cared about was his money and his relative fame.

Richard brushed most of the snow off my back, with a touch that was helpful and not sexual, and took over the chore of getting Alfred inside and headed toward his room. Of course, Alfred was already shouting orders: "Lucy, start making those calls! Eric, my favorite burger tonight! Make sure it's very, very well done! And American cheese! None of that pale crap!"

Eric leered at me as he explained, "He means no Provolone or Mozzarella or even Swiss! Just good ole *Amurrican* cheese!" He leaned toward me and I leaned backwards. Eric continued: "My salt and pepper squid is considered the best in Australia. I can make a prawn dumpling better than anything you can find in Hong Kong. It seems like a simple dish, but it's actually pretty difficult! But does he care?"

I stood stock still, both hands grasping my suitcase, ready to bring it around and sock him with it if I had to. Fortunately, he leaned back, saying, " You bet he doesn't care."

"Fine," I muttered. I walked away from Eric, into the mansion, and crossed the wide great room, past vaulting windows whose view reminded me of just how hard the snow was still falling, past the dormant fireplace, and down a hallway into my room. I'd been forced to spend just enough long weekends here over the years that I felt guilty for taking my luxurious surroundings for granted. Everything was overly polished, overly plush, overly shiny and bright. And this was just one wing of the mansion; another one held a gym, swimming pool, a small infirmary, and guest rooms.

I set my suitcase and bag onto the bed, feeling guilty now for mussing the smooth lines of the bed covers. Ridiculous. I shed my coat, gloves, and hat, but I didn't unpack anything except my company-issued phone. I plopped down into the nearest chair (I usually think of my self as sitting *on* a chair, but with one this wide and yielding, you plopped *into* it) and started dialing. Can't stay out of touch with the global empire, after all. Even on a Friday night (Saturday morning on the other side of the world), there are plenty of money mavens who've given Alfred their ultra-private numbers and are eager to take a call from one of his minions (that would be me) in hopes of making a very profitable deal.

Alfred is an investment banker who advises large corporate customers and governments on their dealings in shares, bonds, and other long-term investments. It could be a large company wanting to build a factory or a government wanting to build an airport. Even at age ninety-two, he works eighty to a hundred hours a week and expects everyone who works for him to do the same thing.

He has seven homes in six countries, never mind that he hasn't visited four of those homes in the past decade, and I spend about three-quarters of my salary for a small apartment in an expensive part of L.A. I'm required to live close by Alfred, and he, in turn, loves to live at the center of "the action," to be seen having lunch with the latest hot action star or arriving at a movie premiere's red carpet with the latest hot model on his arm.

Not that he ever gets anywhere with the model. He's impotent. He made sure to mention that to me early on after he hired me. "It forces me to be a gentleman," he told me, "against my better instincts."

I put up with that crap because I need the money. Previously-aspiring actresses have to take any job they can, and it beats waiting tables, at least for now.

I also knew I had to confront the sad reality that a ninety-two year old man might not have much time left. I had no idea what my post-Alfred world might look like.

After a few hours of wheeling and dealing with everyone from Saudi princes to Chinese tech leaders to Hollywood movie moguls, I was beat. Fortunately, Eric called over the intercom moments later to tell everyone that it was time for supper.

Time for the nightly ritual of humiliation.

I headed toward the too-large dining room. Designed for potential large business gatherings, it was largely a waste of space, with fancy furnishings I feared I was permanently smudging every time I touched them, and far too many mirrors, making a room already too big seem ridiculously so.

I arrived just moments before Alfred and Richard came into the room. They traded odd looks as they approached the table, and gave the impression they'd left a conversation unfinished. I had to wonder if Richard had just performed a medical exam on Alfred. Had some medical concern arose just since we'd arrived? Our resident doc seemed to be keeping a sharper eye on Alfred than usual as the elderly man sat at the head of the table. I sat at his left, Richard to his right.

Eric came in from the kitchen, wearing his stereotypical chef's garb of double-breasted jacket, apron, and tall hat, and bearing a large serving tray. I knew it galled him to be both chef and server, but at least it provided me with a moment of amusement most nights.

His own humiliation, I knew, was serving Alfred's favorite dish, the above-mentioned cheeseburgers, well-done enough that they were crunchy on the outside, with the American -- no white! -- cheese melting down their sides. A plain white bun and pickles and onions were the only toppings, thank goodness. Mayonnaise would've made me gag. A large helping of crispy fries completed the dish.

Now came the moment of my personal humiliation -- acting as Alfred's taster. Eric placed Alfred's plate not in front of his boss, but right before me. As usual, Eric suppressed a lopsided grin; no doubt this moment pleased him as much as his humiliation pleased me.

I never became used to the idea that everyone's gaze fell upon me as I took a hefty bite of Alfred's burger, my mouth having to strain a bit to bite through the crunchy exterior. Some vigorous chewing, a discreet swallow, and still everyone stared as I also sampled the fries. I'd never tell Eric, but at least he made great fries, homemade from real potatoes and just the way I liked them -- crispy and brown on the outside, nice and fluffy on the inside.

We were far past the time when someone would make a joke about how at least I hadn't fallen right over dead. Eric took the plate from me, his amused features altering into a subtle scowl, as if indicating that he was disappointed I was still alive. Thought you'd think he'd know whether he'd poisoned the food or not. And he was the only person with access to it ahead of time.

If Eric hadn't been such a sexist twit, I'd have had more sympathy for him. Earlier in his career, he'd worked his way up through the ranks of chefs in one prestigious restaurant after another. Besides the salt and pepper squid and prawn dumplings he'd touted, his Peruvian chicharrones and other dishes were multiple award winners. But he'd seen too many reality shows where chefs shouted at their co-workers and even bosses, and became well-known for throwing things and hurling curses that ended up being "bleeped" in a number of videos that, unfortunately for him, went viral.

Naturally, Alfred saw some of the more vile videos, liked Eric's "independence," and hired him right away. Which means Eric's stuck here as much as I am, scorching burgers and breading chicken nuggets in the style of Alfred's favorite fast-food joints.

Any sympathy I may have conjured up for him, though, was totally negated by his constant leering at me, sometimes winking at me, which I especially hate because it assumes some sort of shared relationship that I definitely didn't want.

I think of him as a wolf in chef's clothing.

And that makes me think of the *first* memory of my cousin Danny that usually occurs to me, though it takes place later than the second one: the two of us at age fourteen, at another reunion at the same farm where we'd skipped stones across the lake, and him grabbing hold of me behind the barn, commenting on how large my breasts had become (his language was courser), telling me, "I got you now," and trying to stick his tongue down my throat before I managed to trip him into a pile of straw and run toward the house.

I made sure, during subsequent reunions, that I only

hung around my non-creepy relatives, and kept as many of them between myself and Danny as I could.

In my immediate family, though, I was always the "lesser" daughter. My older sister Shelly married her childhood sweetheart, Ralph Connelly, right out of high school. He became a doctor, and she had the requisite two children, one boy and one girl, right away. Our mother always praised Shelly for her and Ralph's achievements, but the most she could say about me was that, "she's ours, too."

The most I could manage was a series of boyfriends, the only serious one being a guy named Ricky Weimer when I was twenty-two. Eyes the bluest blue, luxurious hair, crooked smile that intimated that he saw something great about you that no one else did. The only time I can ever say I'd been "smitten." I'd been dating him for about six months and each of us was dancing around the idea of asking the other about marriage. But one night after dinner we did some bar hopping and Ricky drank too much. I poured him into his car and drove him to his apartment, stayed the night as I often did anyway. Middle of the night he wakes up, still drunk, calls me a whore, shoves me out of bed and dives after me, beating me on the head and shoulders, my sides and breasts.

I protected myself as much as I could, my hands and arms absorbing some of the poorly-aimed, drunken blows. Finally Ricky stopped, sat on the edge of the bed, put his head in his hands, and cried. I still hate that some small part of me beneath my rage felt sorry for him, wondered what I must've done to cause him to act like this.

But it was the rage that guided me across the floor and away from Ricky. When I'd gotten out of easy reach of his hands, I asked, in much more pitiful voice than I intended, "What was that about?"

Ricky's hands fell from his face and he stared at me as if he'd never seen another human who was so stupid. His voice, though, was so calm that it was more frightening than a shout would've been. "You were looking at that guy in the bar."

"What guy?"

"You know, the *guy*."

"*What* guy?"

"I told you, the one at the bar. The one who kept looking at you."

I vaguely recalled an unkempt, scruffy guy about thirty years older than I was who looked my way a couple times. "*That* guy? Ugh."

Ricky rose from the bed, took my arms, and lifted me up, eyes ablaze with anger. "'Ugh' or not, no one else gets to look at you, and you don't look at anyone else. You get it? You're mine! You're mine!" I struggled and pulled myself away from him, and in a few moments Ricky fell back into a drunken sleep. I left his apartment and never went back, part of me grateful that I got out of there alive, another part wishing I'd taken a lamp to his head and tried to crush his skull.

Somehow I avoided the trap too many women fall into. I ignored his calls and texts and finally blocked him entirely. Eventually, I guess, he gave up. Thank goodness he never tried to confront me physically, and that we lived across town from one another and mostly didn't run in the same circles.

You might say I soured on romance after that, three years ago, though not on sex. I've confined that part of my life to the occasional "friend with benefits."

At the end of our shared meal of burgers and fries concocted by a world-class, if creepy chef, Richard announced, "I consulted the county's online traffic and road safety website. The road leading up here is considered officially impassible."

I paused with a french fry halfway to my mouth. "So we're stuck here."

Eric stuck his head in from the kitchen. "For how long?"

Richard said, "Could be days."

I asked Alfred, who was casually wiping his mouth with a fancy cloth napkin, "Can the helicopter come pick us up?" Alfred's corporate chopper always looked big and imposing enough to lead an air assault.

"My dear," he said, a phrase that always sent shivers the length of my body, "in such a storm as this, the helicopter cannot be risked. I planned upon spending a long weekend here anyway. If it's a bit longer, that's no real concern."

Maybe not to you, I thought.

Eric came into the dining room and stood to one side of Alfred. "We have plenty of food. So we won't have to worry about that."

Great. Three meals a day of burgers, chicken nuggets, and fries, with the occasional chicken finger or onion ring for variety.

This was one of those times I just wished I had a girlfriend to talk to. I wasn't about to try to commiserate with creepy chef, nearly-as-creepy boss, or even seems-nice-but-I'm-not-sure doctor.

I pushed back from the table. "Excuse me. I think I'll read a bit before I go to bed."

I felt Alfred and Eric's gaze upon my ass as I headed for my room. At least Richard didn't join in, but then he was seated facing away from me.

At the time, I could never figure out Richard's relationship to Alfred. He was the only person our boss seemed close to personally, and that included relatives, none of which Alfred considered to be the heirs to his considerable fortune. I assumed that closeness came about because Richard kept him healthy, or at least had the patience to treat him for a series of ailments, some of them, I believed, imagined.

He kept Alfred safe in another way. Much of Richard's medical experience had been as a military surgeon. Apparently he was also an expert marksman, and had shown his prowess, and his bravery, when his field hospital in Afghanistan had nearly been overrun by insurgents and he'd been key in fighting them off. That made him Alfred's unofficial bodyguard as well as his doctor. He was the only man in the mansion that I might be able to trust in a pinch.

My plan that night was to relax in my room, sip on a glass of wine, and enjoy the latest super-length George R.R. Martin tome. I always bought the ebook because I feared for my toes if I ever dropped the print version.

I expected the combination of alcohol along with literary sex and violence to lull me toward sleep, but it didn't. The very silence all around became oppressive; I realized that without me noticing it consciously, that I'd heard each of my wonderful companions puttering around the mansion for awhile, then closing their respective doors. It was well past midnight. Meanwhile, images of swirling snow and of drifts climbing ever higher around and over the house, burying it, and me, intruded into my consciousness.

I wanted nothing more than to undress, slip beneath the covers, soak up some warmth, and drift off to sleep. But that wasn't going to happen, not yet.

I considered having another glass of wine. No, that was a dangerous path. I never liked the loss of control having too much alcohol brings about. Memories of Ricky. So. A different direction. Maybe head toward the kitchen for a glass of milk. That sometimes worked.

I slipped out of bed, out of my room, down the hallway and into the great room which led to the kitchen.

And stopped. Stood before the tall windows of the great room, still illuminated by massive chandeliers, and tried to make out whether snow was still falling. I went to one wall, dimmed the lights, and looked into dark skies. Sure enough, slow-moving clouds formed a thick tent over the landscape, and snow cascaded down even harder than when we were making our way up the mountain.

I was staring right into the very reason sleep was escaping me. And sometimes you have to take your nemesis head-on.

I grabbed a blanket from one of the couches and wrapped it around me. I eased the main door open, shivered at the blast of snow and frigid air that rushed past me, and worked to shield my eyes against the rush of snowflakes with one hand while holding the blanket tighter around me with the other.

My sensible work shoes weren't very sensible in this weather, and the snow came up nearly to my knees. Fortunately, it was a dry snow, so my clothing wasn't getting wet.

I paused about a dozen feet away from the mansion. About twice again that distance, the landscape dropped off abruptly, and I made sure I stopped well before that cliff.

I looked up. Windblown snow still fell, errant breezes casting it down in great sheets one moment, spiraling eddies the next. As much as I hated its effects, stranding me on top of this mountain with three men I didn't entirely trust, I had to admit it was beautiful. All around stood trees and bushes that had magically turned entirely white, looking as if they were encased in a protective cover that made all the thin lines of their limbs appear pudgy.

Snow is the only natural phenomenon I know that can turn a noisy landscape, filled with the busy sounds of birds and squirrels and the rustling of dried leaves into a reading room ruled by a tyrannical librarian who tolerates no noise other than the occasional rush of air.

Having faced my nemesis, and found that I could stand against him and even find some good in him, I decided it was time to go in. I tightened my blanket around me once more and turned --

-- And almost ran right into Alfred Fanning!

He stood immediately behind me, also wrapped in a blanket. His footsteps in the snow were closer together and revealed more of a dragging gait than my own. He looked at me with a wry grin I wasn't accustomed to seeing. "I'm sorry, my dear," he said. "I saw you out here and became concerned."

"I just . . . couldn't get to sleep."

"And so you thought coming out here in the cold and the snow would help you sleep?"

I wasn't about to explain how the snow had intruded into my consciousness and that I'd come out here to give psychic battle with it. "I just wanted to see how deep it was."

Alfred nodded and he raised that wrinkled finger again. He reminded me of an actor I'd once seen playing Scrooge in a stage adaptation of *A Christmas Carol*. "Don't worry. One thing about snow, it's not eternal! It goes away eventually, sometimes sooner than we like, sometimes later. Once it leaves, our time up here will come to an end. Everything ends, after all. I think part of you will appreciate the snow even more once its beauty leaves. Everything, everyone, should be appreciated eventually, don't you think?"

"Of course, sir," I said, not certain what I was agreeing to.

"Again with the 'sir,'" Alfred said. "Let's get rid of that, and also end this rather chilly moment, why don't we?"

"Certainly, uh, Alfred."

I kept an eye on my boss, making sure he didn't slip on the way back in. I anticipated that he might try to continue our little conversation once we were inside, but he didn't. Part of me was curious to know what it would've been about, another part was frightened by the prospect. Either way, I was happy when I finally crawled into bed, cocooned myself in as many blankets as I could, and drifted off to sleep, all thoughts of snow fading from my mind.

KNOCK, KNOCK, KNOCK!

The sudden sound at my door woke me instantly. I pulled my bed covers up to my chin and stared at the doorway like some helpless horror movie side character. *I've got to stop thinking about horror movies!* was my first thought.

Another series of knocks. Richard's voice came from the other side of the door: "Lucy, get up. It's important."

I looked at the clock by the bed. Four-thirty a.m. *What the hell?* I got out of bed, opened the door just a crack. Richard looked thunderstruck. "What's going on?" I asked.

"We're meeting in the great room," he said. "Be there quick as you can." With that, he went down the hallway and knocked on Eric's door.

I dressed in the previous day's clothing, looked in the mirror as I ran my hands through my hair, decided to hell with how I looked, and headed toward the great room.

I nearly collided with Eric as he left his room. Apparently the early hour defeated his usual leering and his snarky attitude, because he actually paused and motioned for me to go ahead. My next thought: *He's probably just wanting a good look at my ass as I walk ahead of him.*

Richard stood in the middle of the great room, the continuing snowfall a backdrop through the tall windows. He rubbed his hands together, and his eyes were hooded. He motioned for Eric and me to take a seat. I let Eric pick his spot first, and when he sat at one end of a couch, I sat in an adjacent chair. I folded my arms, crossed my legs, and waited for Richard to speak.

Eric wasn't as patient. "So where's Alfred?"

Richard took in a deep breath. "That's why we're here. Alfred Fanning is dead."

I felt as if time had slowed to a crawl. Richard's arm was rising in a gesture, but it was taking several seconds to travel a couple of inches. The snow outside appeared to be falling but never reaching the ground. I looked over at Eric and he sat there with his mouth agape, staring but seemingly not understanding what Richard had said.

Finally I managed to speak: "What . . . what happened?"

"I was in bed, not sleeping well. I guess I found the idea of being stranded up here more disturbing than I realized. I heard Alfred call out from next door. I knocked on his door, didn't hear an answer. Fortunately he never locked his door. I peeked in, spoke to him. No answer. I turned on the lights and went to him. He wasn't breathing. No pulse. Pupils not responsive. I tried CPR for several minutes, but I knew he was gone."

Eric started to speak, managed only a growling noise, then cleared his throat. "What killed him?"

Richard said, "Don't know. I mean, the man was ninety-two. Overall, he was in good health, despite his awful diet." At a look from Eric, he said, "I'm not criticizing you. He was responsible for his own menu, limited as it was."

I leaned forward. "When do we get the hell out of here?"

Richard indicated the windows behind him. "The snow still hasn't stopped. We can't drive down, and the company chopper still isn't going to risk the trip. The county might risk it if we had someone who was in danger of dying. To take a body off the mountain, and to rescue people who aren't in immediate danger -- they won't do that."

"But you've notified the authorities."

"I'm waiting until I know what killed him."

Eric's eyes narrowed and his voice was clearer now: "What does that mean?"

Richard stared Eric down. "Just what I said. There's nothing else to be done for Alfred anymore."

Eric stood. "I want to see the body."

Richard shook his head. "Why would you want to do that?"

"Why shouldn't I? The man was my employer. He's the reason we're up here on this godforsaken mountain. I'd like one last look at him."

I said, "You don't seem like the sentimental type."

Eric didn't even look at me. "I'll have to look for another job now. I think I'm owed this much."

I expected Richard to push back more, but he just sighed and said, "Let's go, then."

I didn't move. Richard asked, "Aren't you coming?"

The last thing I wanted to do was view a dead body, but some unexpected impulse made me stand and follow Richard and Eric. Richard paused in front of Alfred's door, unlocked it, and eased it open just a few inches. I couldn't quite see inside, given my angle.

Eric tried to enter the room, but Richard stood in the doorway and wouldn't move. Eric tried to push past, but Richard grabbed one of Eric's wrists and bent it in a direction it wouldn't normally move. "Ow, son of a bitch!" Eric said. Richard was ex-military. Eric had spent his life in kitchens. *I'd say Eric's outmatched.*

Richard said, "Alfred wouldn't want to be stared at as if he was on display. And I'm preserving the site."

That set off an alarm in my mind. "Like a crime scene?" I asked.

"Just a formality. Until I examine the body in more detail. I'll be moving him to the little infirmary in the other wing in a little bit."

Eric stared past Richard's shoulder for about two seconds, then with a "Hmpf!" headed toward his room.

Richard looked at me questioningly and stepped back from the door, but didn't open it any wider. He didn't say anything. I thought, *I can't decide which I'd regret more -- taking this look inside, or not taking it.*

I took the look. In the darkened room, Alfred's body lay on its back, with sheets pulled up to his neck and his arms on top of the sheets.

I made myself look at Alfred's face. I haven't seen that many dead people, so I wasn't sure how his features compared. The dimmed lighting set his face off in stark relief.

I'd seen enough. *The longer I stare at him,* I thought, *the longer I put off figuring out how to react to his death. Will I grieve? Will I miss his presence, or just my job?*

"Thank you," I told Richard, though I wasn't sure whether I was thankful at all. Richard pulled the door shut and I returned to my room. My thoughts whirled around as chaotically as the snow until I fell into a fitful sleep.

K‌NOCK, KNOCK, KNOCK!

Again? I didn't even stir from the bed this time. Seven-fifteen. "What is it?"

Only slightly muffled from the other side of the door, Richard's voice: "Come out, Lucy! We need to talk!"

I groaned as I swung my feet onto the floor. "Now what?"

"I'll be in the great room again. Just get the hell out here or I swear I'll come in there and drag you out."

"What kind of threat is -- " I began, but fell silent when I heard Richard knocking on Eric's door down the hallway.

"Dammit," I muttered. Into the same clothes yet again. I skipped doing anything with my hair. Screw that.

Richard and Eric both stood in the middle of the great room this time. Richard stood stock-straight, eyeing me with a stern stare as I approached. Eric had his arms folded and wouldn't look at either of us.

No invitation to sit down this time. Richard said, "Alfred was murdered."

I blinked a couple of times. My throat felt as if it was about to close up. I managed to croak out, "Say that again?"

"Alfred was murdered. I saw clear symptoms of arsenic poisoning. Most likely it was ingested with his food."

I looked at Eric. "Then that means -- "

Eric took a step toward Richard. "It doesn't mean a goddam -- "

Richard reached behind his back and brought out a pistol, aiming it directly at Eric's chest. "Stop right there."

Eric stopped.

Richard pointed the pistol toward the ceiling. "Both of you, sit down."

I went immediately to my earlier perch in a chair. Eric sat in his previous position on the couch.

Richard remained standing, but stuck the pistol into his belt. "So one of you is a killer."

Eric nearly rose from the couch, but a stern look from Richard sent him sitting down again. "It wasn't me," Eric said. He indicated me. "It has to be *this* bitch!"

"Wait a minute," I said. "*You're* the chef. You're the one making all the food."

Eric waved a hand to dismiss that idea. "Then, to state it pretty bluntly, why aren't you dead? You ate part of everything Alfred did."

My eyes narrowed with contempt. "I have no idea, but I'm offended by the assumption that I'm guilty."

Richard spoke up. "Even while you were ingesting the tainted food along with Alfred, you could've been dosing yourself with the antidote. Folic acid is pretty commonly used."

"Maybe among murderers. But I'm not a murderer." I pointed at Eric. "Maybe *he* placed the antidote in the food I ate, so I wouldn't be killed, too."

Eric screwed up his face in a skeptical expression. "Why the hell would I do that? I don't even like you."

Well, at least this little journey has us admitting some truths. "You wanted to take suspicion away from yourself," I said.

Eric leaned back on the couch. "That's a bunch of bullshit. I know I didn't do it."

I worked to keep my voice level. "Well *I* know *I* didn't do it!"

"Enough," Richard said. "If I had the facilities here, I'd take blood samples from you to see if either of you has the antidote in your systems. For now, I have to assume either one of you could've done this. Or maybe even that you worked together. After all, I have to wonder how Lucy could've gotten the poison into the food."

"What's our motive?" I asked, hating that I sounded like some stock character on a crime drama.

Richard chuckled. "Neither one of you particularly liked Arthur. This was a crime that had to be planned for -- it wasn't a crime of opportunity."

Eric said, "So now you're some sort of criminologist?"

"No, but I can use common sense."

"How do we know you're telling the truth about what killed Alfred?"

I stood, but hesitated when Richard reached behind himself again. "Oh, come on," I told him, "you're not going to shoot me."

Richard lowered his hand to his side. "One of you has already killed once. I won't let it happen twice. I've notified the authorities, so they know who the suspects are in this crime."

I said, "At least we can get off this godforsaken mountain and straighten this out."

"Well that's the problem, isn't it? The local sheriff can't get up here right now any more than we can get down. That's why I'm confining the both of you to this wing. That way you have access to your own rooms and to the kitchen. You can even step outside for a little fresh air if you want -- not that you want to for more than a minute or so. I'll stay in one of the guest rooms in the other wing for now."

Eric said, "So you're just having a little vacation, aren't you? The pool and the gym all to yourself."

I said, as much to myself as the others, "None of this is anyone's idea of a vacation. But wait a minute, you're locking me in here with the murderer?"

Eric stood and pointed a finger right in my face. "Listen, bitch, we all know *you're* the murderer."

I slapped Eric's hand down, and when he took another step toward me, Richard said, "That's *enough*!"

Eric, possibly remembering the presence of Richard's gun, stepped away from me. Richard continued, "I don't want any trouble out of either of you. Lock yourselves in your rooms if you want. I'm going to continue my examination of the body. I'll let you both know if I find out anything else."

As Richard walked toward the doorway leading to the other wing, I backed away from Eric. "Where are you going?" he demanded.

I said nothing, but turned and headed toward my own room.

"I'm talking to you! Where the hell are you going?"

As I headed down the hallway, I heard Eric's footsteps behind me. I opened my door, got through the doorway, slammed the door shut. I leaned my shoulder against it as I flipped the lock closed. Only then did I feel the force of Eric's body against that door. And again.

Silence fell. I put my ear against the doorway, trying to perceive whether Eric was truly gone. After a moment, I heard noise from the grand room, perhaps Eric kicking a waste can or throwing some other object across the room.

Safe for now, I thought. *Sort of.*

I knew I wasn't the killer. Which mean Eric had to be.

But wait! What if it was actually Richard who was the killer? I had no way of knowing whether he was telling the truth about how Alfred died. Richard didn't have easy access to the food before I sampled it and Alfred ate it, but maybe he worked with Eric. He could've supplied the arsenic, and had Eric put it in the food, and now he's betraying him. Maybe Richard worked on his own and administered the arsenic to him in a different way, or killed him in a different way entirely.

Too many possibilities!

And either way, I thought, *I'm the patsy.*

I grabbed a chair and placed it tilting up beneath the door lock. I dragged the dresser across the room and pushed it up against the chair. And the only other chair in the room on top of that. I was considering pushing the bed over when Eric started pounding on the door. "Com'on out, you bitch! You've got to confess!"

He's acting for Richard's sake, I thought, *either to convince him he's innocent if they didn't work together, or to put up a good front if they did.*

Eric's pounding ceased, and I took heart. *I can only hope he's worn himself out.* I started across the room, intending to listen at the doorway again.

A much larger crash at the door! The sound wasn't just louder, it was sharper, as if the strike had been applied with more weight behind it than Eric's strength alone could muster.

Another crash, and I heard the tough wood of the door crack slightly. A longer interval, another crash, and an even larger crack appeared. At the third strike, the door's middle section bowed inward at the middle, and I saw light through it.

"Go the hell away!" I shouted. "Leave me alone, you bastard!"

The largest crash yet against the door, and it cracked apart. Eric yelled through the hole, "You can't keep me out! I'm going to wrap my hands around your throat!" He started squeezing through the hole, and I grabbed a lamp and was about to brain him when I heard Richard's voice behind Eric: "Stop that right now!"

"Shit, Richard, make up your mind," Eric said. "Are you in here or not?"

"Lucy?" Richard asked. "Are you all right?"

"So far," I replied.

"I'd like to get you out of there."

"I'd feel a bit safer in here."

Richard said, "I'd like both you and Eric here where I can see you."

I thought for a moment. "Do you have your gun?"

"Yes, but don't be afraid -- "

"I'm not afraid," I said. "I want you to protect me from Eric."

I heard Eric's voice, from down the hall: "I need to be afraid of her! No telling what that -- "

"That *enough!*" Richard said. Eric fell silent.

I moved aside the furniture I'd pressed up against my now-damaged door. Richard pushed it open. He wore a shoulder holster now, his pistol, whatever kind it was (I'm completely unfamiliar with types of weapons), prominently displayed on his left side. Once I was out, I saw Eric leaning against the wall, arms folded, sulking like a child who'd been denied a candy bar.

Richard motioned for Eric to go into the great room. He did, although he took his time about it. He took his now-standard position on the couch. Likewise, I settled into my usual chair.

Richard sat in a chair across from us. He drew his pistol from its holster and set it onto the arm of the chair, covering it with his hand. Again, I don't understand enough about weaponry to know whether the safety was off.

Richard took a deep breath. "Here's an update. I wish I'd had the chance to tell both of you this before Eric decided to turn to violence."

Eric said, "Now wait a minute! If you'd been falsely accused of -- "

"Shut it!" Richard said. I saw his hand tighten on the pistol.

Eric shut it.

Richard continued: "Now. The update. The authorities contacted me just in the last couple of minutes. They've got a specially-equipped vehicle now, and they'll be up here in the morning. I'm going to sit right here, the both of you are going to sit right there. I've taken some medication that will keep me awake all night, and I'll keep an eye on both of you. Just that simple."

Eric opened his mouth, but must've had second thoughts. He didn't utter a word. He leaned back on the couch, folded his arms again, and closed his eyes. Richard stared at him for about half a minute, then turned his attention to me. He raised his eyebrows in a questioning glare. I shrugged.

I wished Richard would at least turn the lights off, to make it easier for me to get some sleep, but I knew better than to request that. No-drowsing medication or not, it would make him more likely to drop off to sleep, and less likely to catch a glimpse of Eric or me if we tried to move. Not that I intended to.

I resigned myself to my fate and closed my eyes, but didn't expect to sleep. Wild scenarios presented themselves, one after another, of possible futures that could rush toward me over the next few hours, all of them involving gunshots at point-blank range, another battle with Eric, or abandonment in the snow. After a few minutes, I gained that other-worldly awareness I sometimes felt when on the transition between wakefulness and sleep. A rescue helicopter swooped down upon us -- too low! -- and crashed into the mansion, and from the flames and debris strode Alfred Fanning's skeletal remains, arms outstretched like a zombie from a horror film -- *again* with the horror film analogies!

Next came that feeling of stepping down onto a stair that isn't there. I jumped, my consciousness snapped back to reality, and my eyes snapped open.

And I saw Eric advancing upon a sleeping Richard.

I stirred myself to yell, but before I could make a sound, it was too late. Eric grabbed the gun from Richard, and stepped back as Richard stood up. Eric pointed the gun at Richard for a moment, but then a surprised look passed across his face. He hefted the gun in his hand, ejected -- is it called the "clip?" -- from the bottom of the weapon, and said, "It's empty!"

Richard took advantage of Eric's distraction to take off running toward the mansion's other wing. Eric chased after him, but didn't catch up. Richard locked the door to that other wing behind him, leaving Eric to pound on that door as Richard looked on through its narrow windows. Finally Eric stopped, but his anger wasn't spent. He turned toward me, still holding the empty pistol in his hand.

He turned the weapon around as he advanced, clearly intending to pistol-whip me. I ran to the opposite side of the couch, telling him, "Stay away from me!"

"Or what?" he demanded, and jumped over the couch. He grabbed me by the shoulder with one arm and raised the pistol in the other. I squeezed my eyes tightly shut and raised my hands to deflect the blow.

Which never came.

I opened my eyes. Eric was walking away from me. He threw the pistol to the floor and sat in the chair Richard had occupied only moments before. Fidgeted in the chair. Stood up again. He started toward the couch again, and I stood firm, determined to fight back this time.

"Oh, get over yourself," Eric said. "I'm have no intention of hurting you anymore, because I need you. I didn't kill Alfred, which means it's either you or Richard, so I need you both in one piece." He grabbed a couple blankets from a pile of them on the couch. He wrapped himself in them and started toward the doorway to the outside. "Where are you going?" I asked.

"For all you care, I'm going to try to start Alfred's car. I've never hot-wired a car before, but I can sure try now. I'm going to meet whoever those authorities are coming up the hill. If I can't start the car, I'll start walking. I'm making sure to tell my version of what's happening before you or Richard tell yours."

I started to tell Eric how foolish that was, then decided, *What the hell do I care about him? Maybe I shouldn't feel that way, maybe I should understand that I need him as much as he says he needs me. He insists he's not the killer, but I know I'm not the killer.*

I'm not about to try to go out there to drag him back inside. Or even caution him to watch out for that sudden drop-off.

About two feet of snow had piled up against the doors to the outside, and Eric had to shove pretty hard to open them. As he stepped away from the building, he left the doors to the outside open, the bastard, and a chill blast of air rushed into the great room. I pulled the doors shut and watched as long as I could as Richard made his way toward the front of the mansion. Once away from the large drift at the doorway, the snow wasn't as deep, but it still meant he had to take tall steps to make any progress at all. Finally he disappeared around the corner.

I went to the doors leading into the other wing of the

mansion. Looked through the windows. Didn't see Richard. *Dammit*, I thought, *now what do I do?*

I returned to the doorway to the outside. *I've not heard Alfred's car start*, I realized. *Is he really going to start walking down the hill in this weather -- in these temperatures?*

Curiosity got the better of me. I grabbed some blankets of my own and wrapped them around me, as I had during my previous jaunt outside.

The instant I opened those doors again, I wondered what the hell I was thinking. The blowing snowflakes felt more like shards of ice against my face. I'm a few inches shorter than Eric, so it was difficult even to follow in his footsteps. Moving forward meant pushing against the snow rather than stepping into it.

I got far enough away from the house to look around the corner toward and see Alfred's SUV still sitting there. *So Eric didn't get it started*, I thought. I squinted against the snowfall and could just barely make out his tracks headed down the hill. *What a fool. He has no way of knowing how quickly those authorities, or rescuers, or whoever the hell they might be, are going to get up here. He's only wrapped up in blankets like I am, and I sure as hell would never attempt it. I'd go off that cliff out there first.*

I began to shiver, and was about to turn back toward the house when that last thought expanded itself in my mind. *I wonder what it would be like, to take that one big step into the darkness, to outrace the snowfall -- to be free of Eric and Richard and the ghost of Alfred?*

But my next thought: *Hell, no! That's the easy solution, and it would mean they all won. I've let myself stand on the sidelines this entire time. That's about to stop. I need to go back in and pound on that door and* make *Richard deal with me and tell me exactly what's been going on here. Or better yet, run down that hill, drag that son-of-a-bitch Eric back here -- maybe push* him *off that cliff, even though I might be killing the one person who knows the truth.*

I started to turn around, despite not having decided whether the mansion or the hill would be my destination, when a pair of arms grabbed me from behind, lifting me into the air. "Now I've got you, you bitch!"

Eric! He'd sneaked up on me, his footsteps silent in the snow. I squirmed in his grasp as he walked us toward the cliff's edge. "I'm getting a confession out of you, or you're going over!"

Exerting all my strength, I slid my right arm between a couple of my blankets and slipped it out of his grasp. I elbowed him in the face and he screamed and let me go, staggering backwards, his hands covering his face. *He has me on strength,* I thought. *I've got to press what advantage I have.* I rushed forward and pushed against both his shoulders. He fell flat onto his back, and I unwrapped my blankets from around my body and shoved them across his head. I jumped on top of him and hit him square in the face. Blood spurted from his nose and he screamed again. I struck him again.

And again! Eric cried, "Stop, please stop!"

A single gunshot shattered the silence. Oddly, the next thing I responded to was how suddenly its report was absorbed by the snowfall and clouds all around, as if we were players on some sort of stage.

I raised myself from Eric's prone form, thinking Richard had re-loaded his weapon and come out to break up our fight.

But when I turned toward the mansion, I gasped, and my knees became shaky. I tried to speak, but my throat felt as if it was closing up.

The person standing there holding a pistol still aimed at the sky was Alfred Fanning!

Alfred, who was bundled up in a thick coat, toboggan hat, and long scarf, lowered the weapon. Richard was standing directly behind our formerly-dead boss. Alfred handed the pistol to him. He holstered it and went over to Eric, who stared between bloody fingers held against his bloody face. "I tink she broke by dose," he said.

Richard lifted Eric to his feet. "Com'on, let's get you cleaned up, then I'll check you out."

I looked at Alfred through narrowed eyes, as snow was still blowing directly into my face. "I . . . I can't believe this."

"My dear girl," he said, and you'd asked me ahead of time what his first words to me after seemingly rising from the dead would be, that's exactly what I would've guessed. "This was all a test."

"A test? Of what?"

"Of *you*, of course. I wanted to see how you'd react in an extreme situation. And despite a slow start, you committed yourself grandly."

I waved an arm to indicate the mansion, the snowstorm, the entire mountain. "All *this*? How could you have planned on this?"

Alfred's lined face grinned up at me. "Oh, not the weather, of course. That was just taking advantage of the opportunity. If the snow hadn't been forecast to strand us up here, I'd have concocted some other situation. Richard was in on the whole thing from the beginning, of course. Despite his military service and documented bravery, he hasn't the drive to run an operation such as mine. So he helped me design this scenario in which you and Eric were locked up together, each of you knowing you weren't the killer -- because you weren't! And there were never any authorities coming up here. Placing the two of you under this pressure allowed both of you to show who you really were."

"I could've been killed!"

Alfred patted my arm, and I fought not to flinch. "Without the ultimate price a possibility, how can someone know whether he -- or in this case, she -- is up to the task?"

"The task? What task?"

"Why, taking over my empire, of course. You know that I have no heirs. So I chose to pick among those closest to me." Alfred chuckled. "Closest to me in physical proximity, of course. I realize that none of you has any real emotional connection to me."

"So if Eric had come across better -- "

"He would've been offered this position. But he chose the path of violence. A wasteful and destructive path. You chose to protect yourself, to survive and to hell with Eric if he threatened that survival. That's the quality I was looking for."

I brushed accumulating snow from the top of my head. "We should go inside. You'll catch your death of cold."

"I doubt the cold can harm me much. You see, I'm already dying. I have only weeks or days left."

"Is it . . . are you ill?"

"I have pancreatic cancer. It's hard to detect or treat early, and it progresses rapidly."

I shook my head in denial, and could only manage to say, "I'm . . . I'm sorry."

Alfred shrugged. "Let's face it, you've pretty much been running things for years. Now you'll be rich beyond your wildest dreams."

YOU'D THINK THAT WOULD BE THAT. ALFRED AND I WOULD return to the warmth of the mansion, sit down like two colleagues instead of boss and minion, and after a time he would pass on and I'd have his empire and all the money that came with it.

Actually, it did pretty much happen that way, but it was a close call. In my anger over the way Alfred had duped me, and risked my life, I nearly refused his offer.

But then came a flash of anticipation, of how exhilarated I'd be to have all that money, not for the reasons Alfred embraced his riches, but to help as many people in this world as I could, people whose life goals, like mine, had been thwarted so often. I'd find my own way to outrace the snowfall, so to speak, but as a way to embrace life, not death.

Now I've achieved so many of those goals -- Alfred wanted those seven homes in six countries, some of which he never lived in; I've opened a string of shelters for battered women in nine major cities, and I visit them all at least once a year.

Alfred savored those red carpet appearances; I recruit the stars who stride down those carpets to promote my efforts against homelessness.

He wanted money mavens to be eager to take his calls and do his bidding around the clock; I convince, coerce, or even shame them into contributing to my drives favoring research into Alzheimer's Disease.

He wanted Eric, a world-class chef, to be ready to prepare that burger with *Amurrican* cheese any hour of the day; I produce a series of TV specials featuring celebrity chefs who promote ways to bypass pirates and thieves to get food to the hungry in Africa. Even Eric has made a comeback on some of those shows. I guess I don't hold a grudge.

We don't talk much, though.

But back to that initial flash of anticipation -- even then, it was *still* a close call whether I accepted Alfred's offer, because his next words and actions brought a different flash, one of remembrance of my mother saying, "she's ours, too," of my cousin Danny grabbing me and sticking his tongue into my mouth, telling me, "I got you now," of Ricky Weimer getting drunk and beating me, saying, "You're mine! You're mine!"

Holding onto that initial flash, the one of anticipation, as tightly as I could was all that kept me from stalking away from Alfred in anger as he grasped me by the arms, saying, "That's my girl! That's my girl!"

ABOUT THE AUTHOR

THE SECRET OF PLAINSVILLE IS DAVE CREEK'S FIRST publication in the mystery field. His other work is largely science fiction. He's the author of the novels CHANDA'S AWAKENING, SOME DISTANT SHORE, and ALL HUMAN THINGS, novellas TRANQUILITY and THE SILENT SENTINELS, and short story collections A GLIMPSE OF SPLENDOR, THE HUMAN EQUATIONS, and KAYONGA'S DECISION.

HE'S ALSO PUBLISHED THE GREAT HUMAN WAR TRILOGY, including A CROWD OF STARS (2016 Imadjinn Award winner), THE FALLEN SUN, and THE UNMOVING STARS (2018 Imadjinn Award winner).

DAVE ALSO EDITED TRAJECTORIES, AN ANTHOLOGY OF stories about space exploration and its many challenges, and is the author of MARS ABIDES: RAY BRADBURY'S

JOURNEYS TO THE RED PLANET, a non-fiction look at Bradbury's Martian stories.

HIS SHORT STORIES HAVE APPEARED IN ANALOG SCIENCE FICTION AND FACT, AMAZING STORIES, and APEX magazines, and the anthologies FAR ORBIT APOGEE, TOUCHING THE FACE OF THE COSMOS, and DYSTOPIAN EXPRESS. He's also been published in the Russian SF magazine ESLI and China's SCIENCE FICTION WORLD.

IN THE "REAL WORLD," DAVE IS A RETIRED TELEVISION NEWS producer.

DAVE LIVES IN LOUISVILLE WITH HIS WIFE DANA, SON ANDY, Corgi/Jack Russell Terrier mix Ziggy Stardawg, and polydactyl cat Hemmie.

STAY IN TOUCH WITH DAVE

E-mail
dave@davecreek.com

Website:
http://www.davecreek.com

Facebook:
https://www.facebook.com/davecreek

Bluesky
@davecreek.bsky.social

If you enjoyed THE SECRET OF PLAINSVILLE, please consider giving it an honest review on Amazon. It's the best thing you can do to help out an author whose work you like!

ACKNOWLEDGEMENTS

"THE SECRET OF PLAINSVILLE" APPEARED IN SERIAL MAGAZINE, September 2019. Copyright 2019 by Dave Creek.

"Sure Thing" appeared in OVER MY DEAD BODY, August 2014. Copyright 2014 by Dave Creek.

"Safe House" appeared in OVER MY DEAD BODY, September 2014. Copyright 2014 by Dave Creek.

"For Lauren" is original to this volume. Copyright 2020 by Dave Creek.

In Plain Sight" appeared in OVER MY DEAD BODY, April 2015. Copyright 2015 by Dave Creek.

"Marlowe, Hit Man" is original to this volume. Copyright 2020 by Dave Creek.

"Beyond Justice" appeared in OVER MY DEAD BODY, December 2016. Copyright 2016 by Dave Creek.

"The Contrary Detective" is original to this volume. Copyright 2020 by Dave Creek.

"Wraiths" is original to this volume. Copyright 2020 by Dave Creek.

"Starting From Scratch" is original to this volume. Copyright 2020 by Dave Creek and Dana Moore.

"The Extras"is original to this volume. Copyright 2020 by Dave Creek.

"The Cleat" is original to this volume. Copyright 2020 by Dave Creek.

"Outrace the Snowfall" appeared in MYSTERY WEEKLY, December 2018

www.ingramcontent.com/pod-product-compliance
Lightning Source LLC
Chambersburg PA
CBHW070932250626
47159CB00009B/3210

* 9 7 8 1 9 4 8 3 7 4 7 7 4 *